I'm Just Like You

By
Hany E Emira
And
Wahid El-Sawah

Translated By: Emad el-din Aysha
Designed by: Abd Elrahman Mohamed

Chapter 1

The aged Brooklyn Bridge sprawls over the East River's estuary. The image of the setting sun strokes the surface of the water as the light begins to fade, leaving upon it the twilight residue of the sky. Purpley reds descending onto the river, turning it into a magical mirror of the heavens. As the silent dialogue between the bridge and the sky and the river proceeds, Fran makes her way across the bridge, after a hard day's work at the department store. She's in pain but she keeps it to herself, fearing the grief that will overshadow the hearts of her daughters, Jessica and Sarah. She was venturing beyond the borders of her world but she felt safe – the old bridge was her friend, where she threw her troubles into the river. She came back, again and again, no matter how lonely the place made her feel, leaving her stranded in distant forests of sorrows.

She was not so old as to feel ill, but the disease that attacked her wiry body was too much for her. How she endured to provide for her children, especially her elder daughter, Jessica, who was studying music and choir at Brooklyn Academy. Fran was not the kind to give up and surrender to the sorrows that always seemed to pursue her since her husband's death.

She was walking weakly on the old bridge, glancing at the sunset with weary eyes, feeling that she had come close to her end as the sun had. She wasn't sad for herself, only for her daughters.

The cold breeze stung her from above the bridge, assaulting her after the sky turned dark. The lights on both banks of the river began to glisten on the surface of the water with their own unique magic. Meanwhile the buildings of New York, off Brooklyn, began to shimmer with their own enchanted azure colours in the waters of the East River

At that moment, Fran was walking, in a whispering conversation with herself, taking tentative glimpses of the sky as she moved along the length of the bridge. Fearing for the fate of Jessica and Sarah, of what time would do to them, the degradation they may face after her departure. She remembered Jessica's dream, how she hoped to complete her studies at the Brooklyn Academy of Music, became a world famous singer or musician. The pain in her soul began to blot out the pains in her body. Her body was being drained and she could feel the end approaching. Her tears came profusely. The dim lights above the old bridge hid them. Only the distant lights of the city that fell on her face shook with the tears twinkling in her eyes.

The moon behind the clouds with its dim cool light also seemed to leave Fran all by herself, hiding as it did behind the New York and Manhattan skyscrapers, obscuring its silvery glow. She had to feel her way along the bridge from her tears that blurred her vision, walking slowly like the blind. She placed her delicate, pale hand on the railing of the bridge to hold herself up; her sea-blue eyes sank down into the river. Gazing at the water and the reflection of the lights on the surface, she could see the image of her two daughters filling her vision, forcing more tears out. She made it to the end of the bridge from Brooklyn, slowly, to make her way to her home on Flatbush Avenue.

After having reached the edge of the bridge, she stood on the main street in front of the bridge until she hailed a taxi. She got into the backseat and told the driver with a low, blunt voice: "Flatbush Avenue please, next to the Brooklyn Public Library." The driver, an African-American, took off. Meanwhile her eyes gazed at houses and buildings with their 19th century meadows, decorated in dark browns with glittering white-framed windows.

The driver, an old man, could spy her sad face in the reflection in the mirror, the remains of tears lying on the corners of her eyes. He whispered to himself: "Seems all those hard days are getting her down." Then he followed her eyes surreptitiously to realize, from his own long experience, that she was passing through a crisis in her life that she couldn't hide. He felt for her, though he had no idea just how much pain she could be in, and he was not so bold as to ask her about her troubles. Even so, he spoke one short sentence: "Take it easy, hon." Then he fell silent. For her part, she nodded in sorrow, grateful for his sympathy. Her hand went to her purse to retrieve the fare, while the driver watched her move her trembling hand as she tried to pay him. He refused to take anything, wishing her well, but she insisted on paying the taxi fare. She got out as he waved to her and left while the darkness of the sky enveloped the city.

She was close to her house now, so she walked slowly toward the garden. Her daughters glancing at her from the porch overlooking the road, worried after the long wait. She was late. Sarah rushed to hug her with her childish innocent smiles, and behind her Jessica. Their arms all interlocked as they dragged her home, singing. But the fatigue was evident on her, which upset Jessica. Taking the initiative, she asked, "What's wrong, mother? You look ill."

Fran replied, "Nothing, dear. I'm just little overworked."

"Then you should rest. Please, Mom," Jessica said. "I won't go to the academy tomorrow and I'll stay by your side. I'll go to the kitchen to get the food ready. Anything you want. I'll cook... pizza, with mozzarella. You have to rest, mother."

Fran insisted, "I'll be fine by tomorrow, Jessica. Don't upset yourself."

Fran sat down, forcing herself to eat the light dinner Jessica had prepared, so as not to worry her daughters. But the pain was beyond bearing. She remembered that day a few months ago that she went to the doctor, alone, without her children knowing. She'd conducted some tests, to learn that her life would set like the sun over the old bridge.

Her mind kept wondering from moment to moment, wondering about the fate awaiting Jessica and Sarah, while Sarah's voice brought her back to them. "Coffee, Mom?" the girl said. Jessica was watching her mother carefully, seeing how Fran was elsewhere, wondering about the mystery that had erased away her usual smiles when she sat with them. She wondered to herself. "What's going on? Where have all those smiles gone?"

After a short silence and the end of a sad reunion, Fran went to her room quietly, to try and sleep while she swallowed down the cries of the burning ache inside her, all the way into the middle of the night. But the pain was too much and she found herself screaming into her pillow. Jessica woke in a start, hearing the cries, waking Sarah up and running to her. They found Fran wailing from the pain, rocking back and forth till she fell off the bed. In panic and confusion Jessica yelled for Sarah to call for an ambulance immediately.

Questions ricocheting in Jessica's mind as she stared at Fran, trying to get to the bottom of what was hurting her mother, to get behind the brave face that her mother had put on, in a futile effort to reassure them. Beautiful Jessica, whose clothes failed to hide the terrain of her slender, lovely body.

Sarah rushed to the phone, terrified and called the hospital, tears in her voice.

Only a few minutes passed before the ambulance came, with its wailing siren that tore through the quiet of the night, standing in front of the house on Flatbush Avenue. Fran was passing in and out of consciousness, spread out on the ambulance stretcher as the ribbon of her memories come to press itself into her exhausted head, again and again. Snapshots of beautiful days past and gone. Playing with her two little girls, with her husband Jack, in the National Park, the green space between the Brooklyn and Manhattan bridges. Afterwards they ate snacks at one of the restaurants on Smith Street, and in the famous candy stores, then read the art and science books, at a publishing house or the Public Library. Then they lazed away after the tour at the Brooklyn Botanical Garden, especially in the days of the Cherry Blossom Festival in the spring, where they played the Japanese drums and filled the place with plays and music concerts.

Her memories of her husband Jack filled her subconscious, which was breathing its last. She remembered her farewell to Jack as he rode the American destroyer heading to the Iraq War, where his life ended in that war after leaving her with their two children.

No one knew what was going on in Fran's mind, laying there, her body drawn-out on the stretcher. But the tremors of her head from the vehicles shivering over the road scattered all her memories, shaking them away as if they were never there. The intervals shrank with time to the point that the past overlapped with the present.

The dawn began to clear the horizon from the aged Brooklyn Bridge as Fran lay on her bed at Brooklyn Central Hospital. With her in Room 7 were her daughters, and a short nurse of Japanese origin.

The steps of the doctor outside the room grew louder and closer, rising the tension in the air. He carried the results of the analysis in his hands, ready to inform Jessica and Sarah.

A fleeting moment as their hearts raced, terrified of the unknown, and suddenly the doctor entered the room to tell Jessica, in a sad, calm voice: "Fran has cancer, and its last stages."

Chapter 2

Scene 1 – The Mother Departs this Life

The white snows falling from the sky on Brooklyn were like the lamps of the angels carrying good tidings to the wishes of mankind. And Jessica was standing behind the glass window of the Brooklyn hospital and her eyes were pleading to the sky, to heal her poor mother, while the faint-throated moan of Fran pierced Jessica's heart and tore it asunder. She turned to see her mother glancing back with her with her last look.

Fran's voice came out, weaker and weaker, called on her two daughters, "Please, don't grieve for me. Let me leave in peace. Don't worry. My pains will end, today or tomorrow."

Sarah's tears fell on her mother's hand as she kissed it, as if they were moments of farewell. As for Jessica, she went back to the window, cluttered with the accumulated snows, staring beyond to the emptiness that ran before her, wondering: "What is our fate once you are gone, Fran? Our father is gone, and now you are ready to leave us too."

The questions escaped her lips like the vapor coming out of her mouth on a cold, frosty night, the sounds of rain drops beating on the window accompanying the snow granules, Jessica turning to Fran once again only to see her mother staring at her daughters' eyes to fill up with the last images she would see of her children. The reel of her memories playing away in her mind, recollecting when she'd play the guitar for her daughters, when they were still little, singing to them. Coming back to the here and now, she took Jessica's hand and placed it on Sarah's, clasping them in her own and pressing while she spoke, "Never let go of your sister Sarah." Then she'd go back to whispering a song from her lips, trembling with weakness, her voice gradually fading as she moaned a long moan before reaching a final silence.

Everything in her fell silent, her breathing, her voice, her movements, everything in Fran came to an end, while Jessica and Sarah, lying on her chest, collapsed, weeping, the sounds of their sobs running through the door of the open room to be heard by the nurse. She informed the doctor who came rushing only to find that Fran had departed.

The raindrops were pouring now on the glass of the window, the white sheets that covered Fran stained now with the tears of Jessica and Sarah, their eyes wandering in astonishment at their loss and the shock of death. The doctor stood silent, placing his right hand on his left in surrender to the power of death.

Jessica had never tasted death before, and burial, and the arrangements that had to be made, as her father had died at war when she was little. She didn't know anything about the procedures that needed to be carried out, but the hospital prepared everything for the funeral, especially since the Fran's family was from Amherst. Her father had died abroad and she'd never met her uncles or aunts because Brooklyn was so far away from Amherst. All that she knew was that her father's cemetery was located at the Holy Cross funeral home. So Sarah went home, exhausted, to preparation the black clothes they would wear for the funeral.

While the ambulance took Fran's body to its last resting place at the cemetery of the Holy Cross, amidst Jessica and Sarah's grief and sorrows. They stood there, draped in their black robes, among the mourners, waiting for their mother to be buried. Jessica embraced her sister Sarah in her arms and said to her, "Please, don't cry, my dear. From this day on I'm your mother." Sarah threw herself into her sister's arms, weeping and stuttering as she collapsed, but trying to hold on while the priest quietly chanted the funerary burial hymns. The undertaker, meanwhile, was speedily trying to complete the burial. Jessica raised her sister's shoulder, ready to leave the cemetery. Nonetheless she stopped for a time to listen to the remaining words of the pastor, sneaking looks at her little sister with her glazed over eyes, wondering about their destiny and the future. She was their mother now, she would have to make all the sacrifices. She would have to forget her ambitions, to sing, her music and studies at the Brooklyn Academy. She would have to work from now on, not only to put bread on the table but for Sarah, who was at to medical school. Sarah was all she had now, and so she made her decision to work, to be like their mother Fran. They were alone now in the world and without someone to support them. In the midst of the sorrows Jessica's dreams were slowly fading away, like little snowflakes falling from the heavens, blown away on a cold winter's night.

Scene 2 – The Mother's Funeral

The thoughts were wrestling within Jessica's head, wild notions and fear over her fate, her eye, confused, darting nervously to and fro as they came out of the cemetery, only for her gaze to fall on a tall man wearing dark glasses standing behind Sarah among the mourners. He'd volunteered some tears during the occasion as Robert remembered those days when he tried to get close to Fran, after the death of her husband. They'd worked together at a large store and, at that time, Fran was full of beauty and femininity, with her slender figure and perfect proportions and her soft, golden hair. Her heart, however, was elsewhere. She still clung to her love of her husband Jack, the officer in the US Navy. She couldn't forget this love, even after his death. And so her colleague's attempts to seduce her, from behind his dark glasses, failed. They met socially, on occasion, often sitting in the cafes of Flat Bush, but only as workmates. They even went to Connie Island with its wooden walkway over the sea, to enjoy themselves, but Robert knew that the only thing she loved in him was his friendship. And so their friendship never turned into marriage, even when he confessed his love to her. She graciously turned him down, saying she was afraid their relationship would take her away from her daugthers. All this despite the fact she was turned on by him, how handsome and attractive she was. She dreamed of him at night, of sleeping with him, but she made it policy to keep her distance in the daytime when they worked together. Now Robert stood, hiding his sorrows behind his glasses, listening painfully to the words of the pastor, and his eyes on Jessica, who was a spitting image of her mother, and on Sarah. Around them were some women, dressed in black, acquaintances and neighbours, waiting for the end of the ceremony.

There were only a few mourners because Fran didn't know that many people and because her hometown was Amherst. She'd become reclusive after her husband died, in grief, a man who died a stranger from his homeland during the Iraq war, dying in the Arab world.

Scene 3 – A Mysterious Relationship

No one knew of this secret relationship with Robert, which oscillated between friendship sometimes and passion and longing at other times, as Fran kept it hidden from everyone, even her two daughters. On one occasion Robert recklessly tried to meet her at his home, away from prying eyes, and tried to make love to her after a prolonged session of seduction, caresses and arousal. She also surrender to his manly power and her own needs, for so long denied since her husband's death. But after all that, with her own manoeuvres towards him, dodgy whispers and touches and some quick kisses that excited him to no end, she insisted once again that they be no more than friends.

The after-effects of the pastor's words still carried on while Robert was knee-deep in his soft memories, but the last words of the priest awakened him from his time with Fran, and he noticed the voice of Sarah and Jessica as they whimpered and wailed. Jessica then turned with her sister, moving slowly, broken now that they were orphans, to face the grave of their mother for one last time before leaving. They would return home but without Fran. As for the priest, he withdrew himself respectfully after completing the funerary hymns. The sun had begun to set, the light in the sky turning a bright shade of grey. Robert leaned towards Jessica and Sarah and kissed them gently to pay his respects. They knew him from his frequent visits, as their mother's workmate. He placed his hands around their waists, walking them to where the cars were to take them back home.

Scene 4 – Jessica Gives up her Dream
Robert's gazes towards Jessica were filled with a longing for Fran, for all his near romantic encounters with her.

Poor Jessica. Her primary concern was her and her sister's future, and how they would pay the daily bills and their mortgage payments and her sister's education. So she forgot her prospects in the world of singing and music. She stopped going to the Brooklyn Academy and looked for work instead. Meanwhile Brooklyn opened its arms to her with all its neighbourhoods, poor and rich alike, in Dumbo and Park Slough----. But what kind of job could she find in those unique places with their exotic dialects and habits?!

The search took her to Smith Street, where the luxury restaurants lay, and the smells of roasting and barbecues. She found herself hungry while there and so she entered a restaurant to have a quick meal. She sat next to an oil painting on her right, while an African American waiter promptly made his way to her. He left her with the menu so she could leaf through it to her heart's content while he made his rounds and came back when she was ready. That's when his eyes fell on her attractive, saddened features, a grief stricken face that hid so much. Now he approached her.

There was no doubt that something of her clung to his heart, but he could not explain it. Was it sympathy, that first step on the road towards love?! Or was it something deeper, a meeting of souls? The end was one, falling hopelessly in love! Jessica was ready to fall in love herself, after what she'd been through. When a woman feels alone in the word, and a bit sad, she needs to be comforted, leaving her on the verge of falling in love at the first hug or kiss and the tender feelings of the man's affection and interest, especially as he felt drawn to her himself.

Jessica felt a strange relief around the waiter, despite his thick lips and dark features that masked a tranquillity and something of the delicious longing that attracts women. Whenever her eyes glanced around the restaurant's walls, witnessing the classic oil paintings on its marble walls, she found her eyes falling on the handsome black waiter, who had the sadness of his people etched on his face.

The man came and went, full of vitality, as if another painting that made up the place. Even with tears that were always on the brink of his eyes, the tears did not fall, as if hanging in his eyes like stars that shone in the darkness of the night sky. It was at that moment that Jessica recollected the mortgage on their home in Flatbush Avenue, bringing back all the worries that her home would be repossessed like what happened to so many in Brownsville.

The image of this handsome black waiter faded from her imagination, as hard as she tried to rebel against her concerns. How his eyes drew her, whenever he wafted in front of her as if he was trying to accidentally call the woman from inside her into the world of love and relationships. She found herself calling on him, "Please." He came closer, stooping a little. She spoke quietly, asking, "Are you looking for any help or an employee?"

Mike sensed that this pretty girl was in distress. He could see it through her grief-stricken features.

Beautiful Jessica, her rosy hued skin, lines of enchanting charm exuding from her, drew this waiter – who was called Mike by the restaurant's patrons – in sympathy with her sad face, a face steeped in feminine allure. And so he replied to her by saying, "It's not easy. We don't need anybody new now But, give me a little time and I'll make some discreet arrangements. You'll have to pass by every now and them. Leave me your phone number, to keep you posted."

The dialogue between them seemed formal, but something needed to be explained by both! Why that mysterious satisfaction between a beautiful white woman, a black man?! Was it the desire to rebel against the rituals of previous generations?! Or was it a touch of love?! Or a renewed love of life?!

Jessica left, running happily down Smith Street, hope once again filling her life with joy, because life was worth living!

She would have been in touch with this young man who'd touched her heart, perhaps unknowingly, but she was ready for it, to fall in love for the first time. To dissolve in its magical world, especially with this young man who would help her out of her sorrows and her need to work. The circle of sorrows slowly shrank from her heart, bit by bit, so that part of her heart returned to normal, flaming with the taste of life.

Chapter 3

Scene 1 – Love or Nostalgia

The grey car was gleaming in the gloom of the Wednesday night, heading towards Jessica and Sarah's house, in a neighbourhood that was badly lit that night. The identity of the driver was not immediately evident to the naked eye… A crime can happen in the blink of an eye… It's none other than Robert from earlier in the day, staring at Jessica's bedroom window while still behind the wheel of the vehicle. He could just spy a light behind the window, witnessing a grief-stricken Sarah and Jessica sitting in the shadows trying to arrange for their expenses from now on.

The sound of the car in the quiet of the night caught the attention of the two sisters. Jessica, startled, made her way to the window to see Robert leaving his car and walking, with quiet footsteps, to their front door. He was smoking a cigarette with supreme authority, a man in is fifties who had sublimated his raging passions into paternal affection. Whenever he remembered Fran, he felt a deeper desire to be true to her memory and felt more sympathy to her daughters who were now alone in the world.

Every single place held a memory of Fran, the past continued to haunt him. He only awoke out of his delirium when he reached the door, only to find Jessica had opened it. "Welcome, uncle Robert," she said.

"Hello Jessica. Hallo Sarah," he replied. "How are you doing now?"

"Fine thank you, uncle Robert," Sarah replied.

Robert entered only for his eyes to fall on where he'd sit, with Fran, when he's visited her to try and be romantic. It all brought back memories. There was the time Fran had snuck out in the middle of the night, in the heat of the summer. They'd met in the garden in the moonlight. He could only see her glittering face and silver curve of her bare chest. She was drunk with love, but nothing happened!

He asked then what they were going to do now that Fran was gone, sadness all over his face.

Jessica answer first, "Don't worry, uncle Robert. I'm going to get a job."

"But what about your education?" Robert replied, startled.

"We need the money", Jessica explained. "And I have to put Sarah through medical school, and there's the mortgage. I'd also like to do some house cleaning. To make a little extra."

He was visibly affected as he listened to her, but what was the solution?!

He replied calmly, "I'll see what I can do." He had some favours he could call in, he thought after falling silent.

Robert seemed to be the real article, sympathetic and caring. Robert the romantic vacated his heart only for the fatherly to take its place. He's never married, after all, thanks to his relationship with Fran.

He resumed the conversation for a goodly time, recollected more and more of their mother, then excused himself, saying it was getting late.

They said their farewells and he said he would call as soon as he found her a job. She thanked him and he left.

No sooner had Robert gone that Jessica's mobile phone began singing its familiar call tone. She rushed to the device and found that it was Mike. "Hallo Mike", she said expectantly.

"Hallo Jessica," he replied jovially. "Good news. Tomorrow, come over at 7am sharp to get your new job, just like I promised."

"Thanks so much, my dear Mike. You'll see me tomorrow for sure," she said with glee. She couldn't sleep all night. Was she thinking about the new job, or something else?!

The first rays of the morning sun began to show themselves, creeping in through the bedroom window. Jessica rose promptly and began to go through the daily motions, preparing herself or her first day at the restaurant to meet her new boss. She took a taxi to Smith Street so as not to be late, her motions nervous the whole time. For his part, Mike waited eagerly for her arrival, not knowing quite why.

The car arrived in front of the resturaunt, at 7am sharp. Mike was there waiting for her.

"Good morning Jessica," he said.

"And the same to you," she replied.

"Quite. Get ready for the meeting. Don't hesitate."

The job interview didn't take that long. The boss was brutally honest with her during the conversation and gave her a job in the kitchen. She glanced at Mike with appreciation and made it home straight away, head over heels, and told her younger sister the good news. She welcomed the news, keeping her tears to herself, sorry for the terrible sacrifice Jessica was making for her. She could feel in her heart the beginning of a new life for the both of them. The following day, Jessica awoke, relieved, the sadness in her eyes making way for something else she didn't quite understand. She put on a blouse and a pair of faded jeans that accentuated her curves and some light makeup and made her way to work. Sarah looked on in wonder. Was it the new job, or something else, that had captivated her elder sister?

Sarah suspected it was more. She wasn't a child anymore and she had her feminine intuition too.

Scene 2 – A Special Kind of Help

Jessica received her job at the restaurant. She had to make pastries, when she didn't know the first thing about them. Mike helped her along the way but even with that she made mistakes, so the boss fired her, until Mike stood up for her and he changed his mind. She kept at her job, under Mike's tutelage and encouragement, supervising her half the time, and training her, the other half. She eventually learned how to make pastries right, making her all the more attached to him, her feelings creeping up on her like the imperceptible crawling of ants, without her even knowing. If wasn;t for her new duties, and worries, in life, she could have been clear headed enough to fall head over heels in love with him and get into a proper relationship. She had all the ingredients of love in her.

It was all in her eyes, those two opals that shone with the light of ages past, the magic and daring-do of stories like *The 1001 Nights*. Her body spoke volumes too, and Mike could hear the din of love. His emotions drew him to her. One particular day he made a rendezvous with her, telling her to came later in the day so he could give her some work advice and let her on some of the secrets of the trade. She agreed, nodding eagerly, then she remembered her mother. Making her way to the cemetery instead of going straight home, she stood in front of her mother's gravestone and spoke. "Rest easy, Fran. Your daughter is going to make it. And Sarah is going to complete her education." The flood of memories caught her unprepared and she cried the rest of the time she was there, Sarah noting how her sister's green eyes were tinged with red when she made it back home. There was sadness in Jessica's eyes, but also hope and something else, so Sarah knew there was a relationship in the offing. And she was glad for elder sister. Let her fall in love and get a boyfriend, anything to help her forget the pain they'd just endured and life to the fullest.

Scene 3 – A Warm Welcome

The last moments of the sunset and the twilight scene covered the sky with a divine mix of charming colours, words for which did not exist in the dictionaries, covering the skies over New York, Brooklyn and Manhattan. The same magical sky above that old bridge over the East River, and over Brooklyn with its homes, with remnants of houses built out of brown stone, with their Bohemians owners from all part of town, like Dumbo and Park Slope Williamsburg, places with their own magic and beauty, drawing in the young, boys and girls, fascinated by these strange houses and their affordable prices. Not to mention the plush open air cafes and bicycle parks. Simplicity in all things. That's Brooklyn, loved by all!

That's when the two young lovers met, at Greenpoint, adding their magic to the magic of the ferry they were riding across the East River----CHECK----. They met like old friends, restraining themselves beyond belief in a climate that edged towards coldness with some tentative drops of water in the air. On either side of the river there were hip joints and Polish restaurants that were chocked full of people after 6pm, when people were finally free of work to roam the streets. And so Mike with his dark, African handsomeness met up with Jessica and their exaggerated friendship turned into something else entirely, a love story in the making with many a philosophical dialogue about relationships and needing each other, not to mention the tortuous link between sex and love.

Did sex make love, or love make sex? Did sex strengthen a tender relationship? He'd ask sometimes but at other times he'd do the answering to his own questions: "It's a two-way relationship. Each gives the other life. Emotion was never enough by itself. No way the relationship between a man and woman could continue by emotion alone, without anything physical between them." And so the conversation extended itself, as if they were building a bridge between each other, an intellectual dialogue grounded in love and compassions. This was the first time Jessica had ever talked about such things. Her face was as innocent as an angel's. But her body said otherwise.

Mike's eyes were roaming over Jessica's rose-tinted skin while a poetry boffin in the background read out verses from Lorca's "The King of Harlem", that section of New York that the whites had graciously left to the blacks, to eke out a living in menial labour.

The Greenpoint ferry was on its way back as the weather turned cold in earnest, so Mike took the initiative and grabbed hold of Jessica's hand, climbing onto the walkway in between the raindrops. Looking at her, he could see how much of a woman she was after all. He was well-read, a wise man despite his years, so he realized that the intellect and intelligence of a woman was more arousing than the body. Especially with someone like Jessica who was full of hidden desires.

It was at that moment that the drums began beating, signalling a parade, helmed by girls from Porto Rico. Tanned and trim and scantily clad, while yet others with luscious curves were dressed in even less clothes, in what appeared to be bikinis all dancing away oblivious in their youth and beauty, 'jiggling' with their coco-coloured skins, while the young danced round them. All proud to be Porto Ricans.

That was the end of the festivities for the two young lovers that day, the day that witnessed the formal birth of their love. They took a cab to Jessica's home, leaving her at the front door, wishing her goodnight, while Sarah spied them from indoors through the window. She'd expected as much. She saw Mike, kissing Jessica's hand in a transparently romantic scene that had nothing to do with mere friendship. That's when the shock happened.

Chapter 4

Scene 1 – Class Struggle

Sarah had seen her sister coming home from the restaurant. She'd spied her from the bedroom window, saw who she was with. The black man she had returned with.

She didn't have anything against her sister having a boyfriend. She's sacrificed so much for Sarah. She'd given up her musical career, education, dreams. She'd agreed to work tables to make sure Sarah could finish medical school. It wouldn't be long before Jessica began cleaning houses, all for her. But there was something that bothered her. Not the colour of Mike's skin. She had no objections to that either. No reasonable person could have any objection to that.

The man in the White House was an African American.

The problem was her own boyfriend, and fiancée, Kevin. *He* would object. She didn't even need to ask him his opinion of who was in the White House.

She remembered one distinct occasion when they were in the canteen at university, having a light meal and some coffee after their load of lectures, and a young man sat opposite them at their table. A black man.

Kevin's face *crumpled* in revulsion.

That was the first time something like this had happened. Innocently she asked Kevin if there was something wrong, if he knew this man and had a problem with him.

"No," he said, leaving it at that.

"Then what is it," a half-grin on her face, trying to tease him into answering. She'd never seen him this way before.

"Nothing," he repeated. "I just never expected *his* kind to make it this far. The descendants of slaves."

She was shocked out of her mind. Amidst the numbness she recollected conversations Kevin had had with her about his family, his noble descent. Then it began to make sense.

They'd lost their land in the south before coming to New York, an aristocratic family of plantation owners for several generations. Before they'd had to uproot, making a new fortune somewhere else.

Kevin couldn't take it anymore. He got up promptly and asked, told, Sarah to come with him.

She tried to argue, tried to explain, but he would have none of it.

What could she do? She loved Kevin and went along, not talking about the incident again. And now she needed him more than ever, with the death of her mother.

She couldn't confront Jessica. Instead she went into the bathroom, sat on the edge of the bathtub, and cried. She knew this decision by Jessica, she could see the way they shook hands and said farewell to each other, would have untold consequences for her. She was torn by her love for her sister and her love for Kevin. The confines of the already small bathroom getting tighter and tighter as she faced down to the hard choices she would have to make.

She'd fallen head over heel for Kevin the first time they'd met. They'd entered medical school at the same time. She'd seen him for the first time, with his distinct aristocratic demeanour, sipping on a cup of tea and was instantly attracted to him. He was handsome and had a determined set to his eyes. It had taken her a long time before she had the courage to go and talk to him.

She could see the future, as if on a projector screen, with Kevin and Jessica's newfound boyfriend fighting and trading swearwords. And she would be at the centre, torn between them.

Only the sound of the phone ringing jolted her back to reality. She could hear Jessica answering. It was uncle Robert. She thanked him for finding her a job, with some families in the neighbourhood he lived in. She would be up fresh and ready at 7am for her new job.

It was settled then. She was going to become a maid.

Sarah made her mind up. Jessica had the right to be happy, with anyone she chose to be with. It was the least she could do for her elder sister.

Scene 2 – Racism

Waking up to a morning weighed down with worries, Sarah got up and ate the breakfast Jessica had prepared for her. Jessica was headed to the restaurant and Sarah to her university. Another pang of guilt.

Following the meal she put on some warm clothes and went outside to walk through Flatbush square. Normally she took the subway to her university but today she felt like taking the bus. She didn't want to be hidden in a tunnel. She wanted to see people, more than ever, going by their daily lives. It would help her forget.

The day felt fresh, the grass covered in early morning dew. On either side of the road were identical houses, each covered with a crimson roof, with identical gardens gleaming in the early morning light like an ensemble of the city before winter began in earnest. The bus came and she climbed aboard, witnessing it all with her beautiful, wide eyes.

A young black man was out on the bare empty street. Another reminder of Kevin.

She got off at her university and resumed her silent worries, observing everything and everyone. She sat close to the windows in the classroom, taking sneak peeks at the outside during the lecture. She saw her classmates in a whole new light. Noticing, more than ever before, just how diverse they were. There were Asians, from Japan and China, Africans, Europeans, Arabs, and some native Americans. Her scientific eye scanned how they interacted with each other.

The following days were the same, tabulating what made people different and what held them together in her little universe. Kevin was the exception to the rule, but he was *her* exception. Her fate. The residue of a past that was not her own but she would nonetheless have to deal with.

Or was there more to it than that, she wondered. The world was shades of grey, but beneath the grey lay fumes and rage. Why was there a place called Harlem if the society was so at peace with itself? The country had elected Obama to the presidency, but how much had it really changed underneath. Maybe Kevin was a reminder of that.

Chapter 5

Scene 1 – Sarah and the Internal Struggle

Kevin was a stark example of the blue blood, a descendent of the aristocracy, evident in his looks and demeanour. That was precisely why Sarah was attracted to him. He lived in a mansion, like the glitterati of Broadway and Wall Street while she hailed from simple neighbourhood in Brooklyn, Flat bush, peopled by the miscreants of society, white and black alike. That was what worried her, his position over blacks, and their marriage was drawing closer. He was a graduate of medical school himself, in dentistry, and it wouldn't be long before he had his own specially furbished dental clinic, and in Broadway again.

The days were passing, faster than she'd imagined, and she didn't know what to do. How would she explain it to him? What if he and Mike met? Different scenarios played themselves out in her head for what could happen. God help me, she thought.

Jessica and Mike drew closer and closer. She had a second job, as a domestic cleaner, and it was showing in her. Her bodily exhaustion. Mike helped her out at the restaurant and that inflamed her feelings towards him all the more. He'd stolen her heart without intending to. Her fondness turning to earnest love, to obsession. She *knew* that this was the man for her, the man who would take care of her for the rest of her life.

The highpoint of her day was meeting him at work, and he could see the look in her eye whenever they met, and reciprocated, taking every available opportunity after work to head off to East River and wine and dine her at the most romantic spot there. The kisses followed, passionate confessions of the need to consummate their relationship. Every kiss helped her forget what she was suffering, how alone she felt in the world. Just seeing her in the silvery glow of the shy moon, shinning from between the skyscrapers, made her all the more desirable.

That's when she told him she loved him, after one especially magical meeting on the river. She simply had to introduce him to Sarah, and she did one night.

"Hallo, Mike. Jessica has told me so much about you," her sister finally said, smiling.

"Thank you Sarah. We're going to meet again. Soon enough," he replied.

Jessica was bewitched that their relationship had gone from mere friendship and sympathy to love and attachment. Sarah was happy for her sister, no doubt, but that didn't ease her worries, about Kevin.

The remainder of the day, Jessica went on and on about Mike, and their rendezvous with each other, and Sarah went along with her sister's desires, listening to her as she helped put her to bed. Jessica drifted off to sleep in her velvety sheets as Sarah helped draw the blanket over her. For her part, Sarah couldn't sleep, her conscience tormenting her for the ordeal Jessica was going through for her.

Scene 2 – A Racist Incident

One of the news channels on television was broadcasting a story about a black youth, who'd been gunned down by the police. It reminded Sarah of Kevin, of when she'd visited him in his mansion for the first time, a man descended from plantation owners. The mansion itself which was built like a plantation.

Meeting John Meir, Kevin's father, she hadn't comprehended, straight away, how steeped Kevin and his family were in the past. In the pomp and glory of the super rich and their esteemed traditions.

John Meir, like his ilk, wanted to impart all of his traditions to his son and make sure he was just like him. Kevin's house was a museum, full of oil paintings and naked statues, and memories of the superiority of the white man over the black man, turning him into an agricultural worker and a servant, something for the white man to brag about.

Kevin's mother, Catherine, was no better, with her Aryan extraction she behaved as if she was descended from the royal family herself.

The place reeked of the past, whether you liked it or not. There were bronze and brass statues, coaches everywhere, and embroidered silver platters, a conical staircase, a huge classic piano, the marble fireplace greedily consuming pieces of wood, classical chairs, old grandfather clocks decorated in gold and silver… the spell was broken when Sarah heard Jessica moaning in pain in her sleep. Sarah ran to her, saw her placing her palm on her forehead. "What is it?"
"Headache. A terrible headache."
"You sure it's nothing more," Sarah replied.
"Nothing, really. Just a headache."
"You're wearing yourself out at work," Sarah said.
"Never mind. The important thing is you, you're in the fourth year," Jessica explained.
Sarah drew closer, touched her forehead gently and kissed it before heading to the kitchen to make her a cup of herbal tea. That and some aspirin would do the trick, she was sre.

Returning with the cup Sarah found her sister watching the news channel, seeing the mother of the young man who was killed by the police. The woman was screaming to the winds for justice.

Any half-decent person couldn't help but be moved. Whole nations would be moved by what they saw. The next image was that of President Obama, commenting on what had happened, sadness plastered all over his face, especially since the incident had taken place in his state.

Jessica had straightened up to take another drink. Sarah felt compelled to say, "There is a real crisis."

Still recovering from the headache, Jessica replied, "But it's just an isolated incident."

"Well, I'm afraid it'll escalate," Sarah insisted.

"I'd don't think it'll get that bad," Jessica responded. She took another sip them added, "Don't worry, sweetheart. That's get some sleep. We both not get up early at 6 on the morning."

Scene 3 – A Celebration and a Tragedy

An obscure morning as the biting cold portended well to some people, the creative artists who liked adverse circumstances, walking with the cloudy skies above them, the air pregnant with potential. Just the kind of ambiguous beginning that artists' drew on to create their works. The streets were still asleep in Brooklyn, lazy and not eager to rise. Only a few old people braved the streets, slowly, or some young students heading off to their universities here and there, and a poor brown-skinned Porto Rican heading off to work, humidity fuming from their mouths in the early morning chill.

The US flag was flapping in shopfront windows and at official buildings, evidence of a deep and resounding patriotism on the occasion of the Fourth of July. Meanwhile Sarah was headed to the subway, part of her daily routine while heading to her college. She had the morning paper with her, checking out the headlines that announced the final end of hostilities in Iraq and the withdrawal of American forces. It all brought back bad memories, of her father's death, memories she couldn't put behind her that day till she found herself at her university. She found her friend Sandy waiting for her there. They teamed up and went to their first lecture. Later in the day, after finishing their classes, they went to ---- park, only to find groups of young black men, protesting the killing yesterday, with fiery speeches being made.

Every one of the speech makers was a natural born leader. You could feel it. Sarah and Sandy were both transfixed by the display. One of the youths was speaking like the great civil rights' leaders of the past. He began, quietly,

------: "My friends I am speaking to you today with a heavy heart, after what happened, this tragedy we are living in our beloved country, and the struggle that is still going on, threatening the country with division. When will the bloodletting stop? When will we stop paying the price for the stupidity of a few? When will we live as free men, in justice and equality?

"We are all losers, my friends, and our nation is the first loser, paying the price of all the blood that will be shed by black and white alike. Slavery is over and done with, and anyone who thinks otherwise and wants otherwise is a lunatic. I ask, why is it that we are confronted by violence? Blacks and whites? Aren't we all human? Aren't we all defending our great country, working and building?

"Aren't we all contributing, each in his own way? Don't we all have families? Don't we all want the same things in life? We are all losers, I tell you. I see, in the distance, that great statue that came to us from France, carrying in its hand the flame of freedom. The statue itself is the statute of 'liberty'. This land is the land of freedom, the land of justice for all, black and white.

"It's at times like these that I can't keep my tears on the inside, remembering those who weep for the black man who was killed yesterday, his loved ones who will never see him again. I remember him, drowning in his own blood, breathing his last breath. His face, I can see now in front of me, as if it's asking: until when? When will this continue to go on? I also couldn't help but shed tears when I say black kids going up to the police, the white men, embracing them, wishing this had never happened. Again I ask who is the winner in all this, stocking the flames of hate and fear between us? I call on you, once again, not to let the past catch up with you and drive us apart in our land, the land of freedom and equality and justice for all, regardless of race, religion or creed. America isn't just a plot of land we're living on. It's in our blood."

Now everybody in the university was listening to the speech, as if they were witnessing Frederick Douglass himself making his famous abolitionist speech on independence day. More and more people gathered and not soon after they were shedding tears like the speaker, black and white together dribbling raindrops onto the ground.

Sarah and Sandy were crying like the rest, then Sarah caught the scent of Kevin's cologne

Chapter 6

Scene 1 – Love Confession

The days past and Sarah entered her fifth year in medical school while Jessica became a well-known domestic cleaner following her mother's death. Hardly a day went by without her heading off, in the evening to some wealthy person's house in the posh parts of town to consummate her duties. Not that he enjoyed herself at night. It was only when Mike was with her, at the East River, that she enjoyed the nightlife. When she had to work, however, it meant pushing her body to breaking point, and having to endure lurid looks or worse from some of her employees.

She'd return home, the colour gone from her face. When she'd look in the mirror she'd hardly recognise herself. Was this really her, with those worried eyes and tired features. How cruel you are, life, she would think to herself. She wasn't her beautiful self anymore. The only thing that lifted her spirits was a song, and she's often find her sister Sarah singing along with her, only for Sarah to beg her forgiveness afterwards, for being responsible for Jessica's lot in life. For taking her dream away from her, to be a musician and a singer.

"Don't worry," Jessica would say. "It's not long before you graduate."

"But you gave up your dream, your happiness."

"I've found my happiness."

"Where?'

"With Mike."

So, Sarah said in turn, "And I've also found my happiness, with Kevin."

They hugged in a moment of happiness while having a light dinner before heading off to bed. The lights went promptly off and Sarah fell sound asleep. Jessica, however, couldn't. She was haunted by her memories, of when she was at Atlantic Avenue, at someone's house, doing the cleaning. As soon as the wife was out of the house the man who owned the place tried to take advantage of her, drawing close to her, ever so slowly. He tried to sweet talk her into his embrace and she just ignored him, which only made things worse. Part of her job involved kneeling over, bringing out how round her backside was and how long and shapely her legs were. Climbing up the stairs or cleaning the shelves from a ladder was even worse, giving him the opportunity to stare up her skirt.

The man, in his feverish mind, was fantasising about having a 'relationship' with her, such a young and beautiful girl. After she was finished, coming down the stairs, he made a grab for her hand. She tried to break free but couldn't. He embraced her and tried to rip her clothes off, pinning her to the ground as she screamed. It was only then that the man's infant daughter, startled by all the noise, began screaming, "Daddy, daddy!"

The little girl was running to him from her bedroom, just barely giving Jessica the chance to break free from underneath him, making it out of his house. She put herself to order again, resuming her composure despite the streams of tears running down her cheeks. She quickened her pace, wiping the remaining tears from her eyes.

The ghost of that night was still with her, the barbarism of that man who was more animal than human. It was destroying her resolve. She never breathed a word of this to Sarah. She didn't want her feeling even guiltier than she was. But she couldn't help but ask herself. Until when? When will I stop having these nightmares?

Then a voice came to her, a deep, booming sound that said, "Until Sarah graduates and marries."

Jessica looked around her to the origin of the voice, but found nothing. She tried to make herself go to sleep, to forget what has just happened, and the nightmare before, just to get a few minutes of sound sleep.

Scene 3 – Sarah Falls Ill

The nigh passed quickly and the Brooklyn morning was upon them, extending from New York to Manhattan, ushering in the morning rush hour as the sunlight reflected off the skyscrapers. The sun also shone on the not so glamorous houses in Brooklyn.

The alarm went off, waking the two sisters, but Sarah got up slowly. Her body was tired and her head hurt, all the hallmarks of a bad cold. She had to stay in bed. Jessica left some medicine by her bedside and a light breakfast, having to leave for work. Sarah stayed put, her body aching. Lazily she turned on the TV set. The news, but she couldn't concentrate. All she could think about was Kevin, how he'd react to her not being at university today. They saw each other every day, attended many of the same classes, and then went out after class. They spend a wonderful time with each, heading to all sorts of wonderful places, and sometimes head back to his place, the mansion, and really enjoy themselves like the young invariably did.

She put her hand to her head, in pain and in boredom, coughing. She wasn't used to being by herself. She was always doing something, with someone. Especially in the daytime. Something else she missed, in Manhattan, was the chance to see a group of black students to revive the memory of Marcus Garvey, chanting poems about their African heritage, with the police looking on, providing protection.

At the same minute, Kevin was heading off the medical school, with its front entrance that was the colour of the sky, and the floor on the inside that was decorated like a checkerboard, and the lovely garden on the outside, surrounded as it was by a wall of granite blocks. Normally, when Kevin was here, at this time, he'd find Sarah waiting for him, with Sandy and Ray and a group of friends. He found the group, as planned, but Sarah wasn't among them, although they were all scheduled to go to the museum of modern art.
----check address------
Startled, he asked Sandy where Sarah was.
Nervously she answered that Sarah was bedridden, sick with flu. He didn't waste any time and phoned her up. She replied, voice still feverish and apologised to her sweetheart, insisted she'd be in tomorrow for sure.
"No problem" Kevin replied. "We'll postpone the visit to tomorrow then. I'll be over in the evening to see how you are doing."
"I'll be waiting," she replied cheerily.
"Till we meet then."

Scene 3 – Portrait of Passion

Jessica made it late to the restaurant that day, and Mike, for his part, was worried sick about her. Whenever she wasn't around him, he didn't feel himself. His passion never abated. When they met, it was like the waves hitting the shoreline anew.

When they worked away, on Smith Street, that poshest of posh places populated with fancy restaurants and cafes, their conversations were always abbreviated. That's all that work allowed for. It wasn't nearly enough for either of them.

This time around Mike learned that Sarah was ill, why his beloved Jessica was late.

"How is she doing," he asked.

Jessica said she would be okay but she was still worried, because the exams weren't far off.

The voice of their boss rang out for them to get back to work, but Mike, defiant, promised that he would come over in the evening to see how Sarah was doing.

It was the least he could do, for Jessica.

Chapter 7

Scene 1 – Sarah and Kevin's Love

Sarah was so mad for Kevin she hardly kept anything from him, especially during their many romantic randevous. Their lovely outings, in Manhattan and the entertaining parts of New York gave him ample opportunity to find out so much about her, especially what happened to her after the death of Fran, and Jessica's sacrifices for her sister. How Jessica, who'd inherited her mother's musical talents, had given it all up for Sarah, cutting her own education at Brooklyn academy short, all so Sarah could become a doctor.

Consequently, Kevin appreciated Jessica's role in Sarah's life, and Sarah quite naturally told him about Mike and how important he was to Jessica. She just left out one minor detail!

Scene 2 – A Fated Meeting

The sun that day was on the verge of setting, despite its passionate embrace of the Statue of Liberty, giving it a lovely redish bronze colour enlaced with a faint golden sparkle. The sun finally sank into the Atlantic Ocean while Kevin made his way to Jessica's house, driving his car over Brooklyn bridge to Flatbush Avenue to check on Sarah. The journey was a trip down memory lane for Kevin, having visited old Brooklyn in his youth, with his father, before the man had turned terribly ill. Kevin took his time, crossing many a street he didn't need to, just to see what had happened to the town after all these years.

Brooklyn wasn't as marginalised as he remembered, when his father has taken him on a formal occasion, visiting their friend Thomas, who'd just won a seat in the Congress for Fort Green and East New York.

Kevin's head almost floated up in the air thanks to the memories moving around in it, the potent scent of the cigar he was smoking filling the car along the way. Brooklyn, an urban morass that had, once again, changed its colours.

His hand snuck its way to his mobile phone to make a call Sarah. "I'm on my way, be there in a couple of minutes."

Sarah expected as much and had tried, with a little help from Jessica, to doll herself up. It wasn't easy with the fever she was running but it was worth the effort. The makeup and the jewellery helped hide her state of health, only just. Then it hit her.

Mike was on his way too!

Jessica didn't seem to mind. "It was bound to happen, sooner or later," she said. That's when the doorbell rang. Jessica's opened the front door to find Kevin greeting her. She invited him in.

Sarah got up, in a start, to hug and kiss him, still in her weakened state, and hiding her worries about what was to come. He reciprocated, while eyeing her carefully, noticing the tension in her.

Jessica left the two love birds to their own devices and busied herself with making coffee for everybody, excusing herself to head off to the kitchen while Kevin sat himself next to Sarah to shower her in gentle kisses. Moments passed and Jessica returned while Sarah waited, anxiously, for Jessica's home to ring its distinctive ring, signalling Mike's arrival. The mobile rang!

"We're waiting for you," Jessica said.

"That must be Mike," Kevin said. He'd heard so much about him he was eager to finally meet him.

"You'll see soon enough," said Jessica, with her feminine allure.

Sarah almost spilled her coffee when the doorbell rang. That's Mike alright, she thought.

Jessica hugged Mike and kissed him before he had a chance to say anything.

"So this is… Mike," Kevin said, after Jessica's guest finally fell into view.

Jessica's voice waivered from excitement as she introduced him. Kevin, just looked on, a look of disgust slowly making its way over his features.

Mike, not noticing, extended his hand to say high to Sarah's boyfriend. Ignoring him, Kevin made his way to the bar instead, to fix himself a stout drink.

Jessica was frozen like a statue of ice, embarrassed out of her mind. It took some time for the blood to move in her veins once again. She went after Mike, to calm him down, noticing how she was tracing his steps backwards a bit after what had just happened. He was realising that he was an unwanted guest here as Jessica placed her hand in his and drew him back to her. He was beginning to sweat as Kevin lit another hand-wrapped cigar, the lit tip of the cigar shivering along with his hand. He turned his back to them to fix another drink, the sound of the ice cubes clinking away audibly in the glass.

Mike took the initiative, biting his tongue as he said, "I've heard so much about you, I've always hoped we could be friends. Especially since we're going to be related not too long from now."

"That's no concern of mine," Kevin replied. More ice cubes made their way into his glass.

"Let's shake on it," Mike said.

"I don't know you," Kevin said, without moving a muscle.

"Is that so," Mike replied. "But you know my race, and I know you too. You're kind, and how you feel about us."

"The way I *feel* is none of your business," Kevin said. "I decide what I like and what I hate."

"I'm sorry, love is not part of your vocabulary. You won't even shake my hand." Mike paused before adding, "A civilised man like you should read more. Read *Roots* by Alex Haley, or -----. That' what'll make you civilised, and make you know what love is about. And how you can love someone, forgive them, for what their ancestors did to your ancestors."

Kevin fumed on the inside. "My ancestors built this country," came his abbreviated reply.

"You did it with our help," Mike retorted. "It was our sweat and blood, and the crimes of your ancestors, on the coast of Africa."

"I don't have to shake your hand if I don't want to," Kevin said defiantly.

"True. But you didn't give me the honour to shake your hand, a privilege I don't deserve."

"I'm not responsible for what my ancestors did and nobody appointed you to judge me," Kevin said arrogantly.

"It's called being *humane*," Mike said calmly. "Values you don't aspire to. The law may not punish what people feel on the inside, the hate, but history will judge."

"That's a privilege you don't deserve," Kevin said in an effort to keep his anger under control. He wasn't successful.

"People like you," Mike said smugly, "are turning the clock back."

"History doesn't concern me," was Kevin's reply.

"Does God not concern you? He created us this way. Are you saying He made a mistake?" Mike threw back at him. "I'm just like you, my friend. a human being. I breathe and eat and sleep, just like you. And my blood is as red as yours."

That's when Mike finally lost his cool and made for the door.

A pang of conscience tugged at Kevin as he listened to those impassioned words, but he silenced it as Jessica rushed out to catch Mike before he left for good.

Mike said he would be fine and asked, told, Jessica to go back inside. "I want to be alone," he said.

"No, I won't," Jessica said firmly, calming him down the best she could.

They left together, hand in hand.

He remained quiet the whole way back to his home. All he was aware of was the sweat on his brow. Even her tender kisses didn't register, till they were at his place.

He threw himself down on the closest chair, exhausted out of his mind, then broke out in tears, face between his palms. Jessica meanwhile prepared two glasses of champagne. She sat next to him and placed her arm around him, offering him a glass.

It had no effect. She made her mind up. She would have to stay the night. She couldn't leave him like this. She phoned Sarah and told her.

It was at that instant that Jessica realised that the only solution was her body, it was the only balm for his wound. She pealed her clothes off and they melted in each other's embrace, forgetting everything in that moment of passion.

There are times when sex is like wine, helping you forget your pains if only for an instant.
Sarah hadn't expected Mike to be so impassioned and so eloquent in his responses to Kevin.
Kevin? She was furious at him. He had no excuse in the world for the way he behaved.
"How could do that to him" she said. "You hurt him, and Jessica. And me."
"You know what I think of his kind," he replied all too easily.
"That's your problem. Mike is my sister's guest, and mine."
"You didn't tell me he was black," he replied.
"Is that an 'issue' worth mentioning? Don't you know what century it is, or who they elected president? And Jessica and her love are none of *your* business."
"He said they were getting married."

"Is that it?" Sarah said shrilly. "You're afraid our bloodline will be polluted? Well, I'll have you know that Jessica loves him, is crazy about him, and nothing will prevent her marrying him. Doesn't she have the right to be happy, after all she's done for me? You wouldn't believe what she was like before she met him, straight after mum died. It's her life and I have no say over it, and neither do you."

She paused for a moment before surprising herself when she said, "Kevin. I don't think we're going to be happy together if you insist on being this way."

He didn't know what to say. Anxious and agitated, he got up and promptly left without a word, taking his car and heading straight out of Brooklyn, her harsh words ringing in his ears. The only thing that would drown them out was more liquor, and so he went to a hotel in a seedy part of town and downed several drinks at the bar. There was no shortage of skirts there, of every colour and size, to help him forget.

He spent the rest of the night there, between a bottle and a gal.

Chapter 8

Scene 1 – Betrayal

Kevin drank like a fish that night. His mouth felt like one of those old wooden beer barrels, the stench of alcohol pervading it. he kept on drinking till one of the girls there took him up to a room, practically had to drag him up the stairwell step by stubborn step, placing her arm over his shoulder to help him up. She shut the door behind her with an expert kick of her heel before she dumped him on the bed and proceeded to undress.

"What's your name, sweetie?" he managed to say.

"Janet," she said expectantly.

Sex was her profession and even in his hazy half-awake state, he couldn't help but be impressed with her body.

The drink had the required effect of erasing the bitter memory of what he'd just endured, at least with Mike. Janet's seductive moves helped him forget everything else.

Scene 2 – Kevin's house is Burgled

It was 4 in the morning when he finally came too, a beautiful naked girl lying next to him.

The place was as quiet as can be. Everyone was doing the same thing as him, recovering from a night of sexual gymnastics. Why else would someone frequent this place, unless they were trying to run away from something.

That's when Kevin's mobile phone exploded into life. It had to keep on ringing before Kevin finally answered it, the liquor finally beginning to wear off.

It was his mother. She was distraught, crying. Screaming.

"What is it? What happened?" he yelled back.

"We've been robbed! Somebody broke in yesterday. You always leave here by myself, me and your bedridden father. Get back here and fast."

"Are *you* okay," he asked, startled.

"Yes, I'm fine. But the house…" her voice trailed off.

He got dressed in a rush, leaving Janet to her own devices, and made a run for it, driving frantically back home. It was only by the graces of God that he didn't crash into a car along the way.

He raced over the fence and ran into the garden till he got on the inside and rushed up the stairs to his mother's room. He found her collapsed, shivering all over.

"Where's Rita," he asked, referring to the maid.

His mother, Catherine, answered that Rita was asleep in her room when all this happened. His mother berated him for not fixing the alarm system, as he should have, or else the burglar couldn't have got in without making a sound. "He got in here while I was asleep and broke into the safe and stole my jewellery, all of it." That's when she woke up and realised what was happening, and grabbed hold of his arm as he made a run for it. Ahe screamed and screamed, digging into his arms with her nails, and scratching him badly, she explained.

She was sobbing from fear, and sadness, now. Kevin, trying to remain calm, asked his mother to describe the man.

"He was wearing a mask and I wasn't wearing my glasses anyway. But... I think he was black."

Bile rose up in him when he heard those words, and he made a false cacluation in hi head, who else could it be, he asked himself.

He rushed to the phone to call the police. A few short minutes later and they were there, with an ambulance to take care of his mother. With Kevin's help, the policeman in charge made his way to Catherine's room and questioned her on all the relevant details.

After getting her statement and surveying the crime scene, he asked Kevin how much was stolen.

He answered as mother had told him then Catherine explained how she'd dug into the man's arms and cut his skin.

"Good," the policeman said. "Then we can get a DNA sample."

There was one more question though. "Do you suspect anyone?"

"Mike," he answered without hesitation.

"And who may Mike be," the policeman said, noticing the ease with which Kevin has answered.

"Someone who works at a restaurant, in Smith Street. That's all I know about him," Kevin replied.

"And why do you charge him?" the officer said.

"We had… an argument," Kevin explained. "Let me put it that way."

"Is that enough, in your opinion" came the predictable query.

"Yes," Kevin said with certainty. "I'm accusing him, and him only. I'm sure of what I say."

"And where were you at the said time," the policeman continued.

"At a bar."

Another question directed at Catherine. "There was no one else with you in the house?"

"Just Rita," she said. "And my husband, but he's incapacitated."

It was at that point that Rita entered the room, with the coffee. She was of Mid-Eastern extraction.

"We'll take him in for questions and proceed with the investigation, the officer explained.

He left, unconvinced of Kevin's justifications, but he had a job to do and his next stop was smith Street. A few casual inquiries and they knew who Mike was and where he worked and his description. Not long after and the officer was in the restaurant, speaking to Mike's boss and informing him of the charges that had been made against one of his employees.

The manager was distraught, worried about his establishment's good reputation. Quietly he showed the officer to where Mike was working, in the kitchen.

Mike and Jessica were busily making sure the breakfast meals were being made right, only for Mike to find the officer in the kitchen with them, explaining to him what he was charged with and by who.

"There must be some confusion," Mike said, startled. "I didn't rob anybody."

"And where were you at 3am?" came the question.

"At home!"

The officer repeated the charge and Mike repeated his denials.

"If you're innocent, you'll be cleared by the investigation. In the meantime, 'm going to have to as to come with us," the officer explained gently.

The whole time of the conversation the officer was glancing casually at Mike's arm. He couldn't help but notice that it wasn't injured. The two policemen with him took Mike by the arms, cuffed him and dragged him with them to the police car, Jessica in a state of shock that had left her dumb for the whole occasion.

It was getting close to 3pm, when Jessica finished work. She asked her boss permission to leave, heading to the Brooklyn police station. Then she found the arresting officer and introduced herself explaining that she was Mike's fiancée. He repeated the charge's Kevin had made but reassured her that there was a DNA test being made and that it would have the final word.

She then told him where Mike had been last night, where she had been with him, and insisted he write down her statement and list it as evidence.

He obliged her quite willingly.

She explained that they'd spent the night together the whole night, and woken up early in the morning to head off to work together.

It was at that moment that the DNA analysis came in and it confirmed that mike was completely innocent. The officer smiled and gave her the good news. "But he can't leave just yet," he added. "We still have some procedures."

The remainder of the time they were there seemed to extend indefinitely till they finally like Mike go. They went out into the streets, running like children, arm in arm, hand in hand.

The sun was setting, the skies turning grey, but it felt strangely warm nonetheless.

"That's go for a walk, and move those lovely legs of yours around Manhattan," Mike said.

Jessica nodded her approvals and added, 'Let's walk all over the country, if you like!"

Mike caught a taxi and asked him to take them to -----------------.

Everything was shiny and clean in Manhattan, everything a work of art, from the skyscrapers to the giant billboards that lit the skies to the fancy shopfront windows to attractive young people walking the streets.

All the lights of the city teased your eyes, blotting out the dying embers of light in the sky hidden behind the grey clouds, turning the clouds purple in their glow.

That was Manhattan, a city that embraced everybody, even strangers to town, like they were long lost friends.

They finally got out at Central Park----check----, moving away from the lights of the big city, departing from the glances and prying eyes of old and young alike. They threw themselves down on the carpet of lush, green grass, exhausted, and proceeded to hug and kiss each other. Then they d, staring deep into each other eyes, before resuming their hugs and kisses, which lasted longer this time.

Drawing back from him, Jessica could see the sadness entering his face once more, recollecting what he'd gone through, the indignity.

"Was does he hate me so," Mike finally said.

Jessica could feel his pain. "It's over and done with," she consoled "Tomorrow, it'll be as if nothing happened and we'll go on with our lives as planned."

"Kevin is…"

She didn't let him complete the sentence. "Never mind him. Think about us. We'll never be apart again."

"For you, I'd stand anything," Mike replied.

They let their imaginations run wild, forgetting the reality around them as they embraced and kissed one more.

On the way back from Central Park, Jessica's phone rang. Whispering to Mike she said, "I's Sarah. She must be worried about me."

Answering the call Sarah explained that she'd just got back from university but hadn't found her. Jessica said she was on her way home and that she had been with Mike the whole tie, and she'd explain exactly what happened when she was home.

Mike remained calm on the trip back. Jessica had helped him overcome the ordeal. The love of her warm heart had done the trick.

They reached -----, getting out of the cab only to find Sarah out in the garden waiting for them.

"Where were you," Sarah said with her nerve-racked voice.

"Let me get inside first and I'll tell you," came Jessica's jovial reply.

Sarah served them some rinks after they'd got in and sat down. That's when Jessica went into detail on what Kevin had done to Mike. Sarah sat there awestruck, her mind reeling from the implications, how could she live with such a man? Someone who's heart is so full of hate?

That's when she took her decision, hand shaking as she picked up the receiver to call Kevin.

Without so much as saying hallo Sarah blurted out, "Why are you destroying everything between us? There's no room for love in your heart. It's over between us."

Her voice was filled with tears, while Kevin was too tongue-tied to reply.

Before he could collect himself to say something, she shut the receiver in his face.

Chapter 9

Second 1 – Kevin's Addiction and Blackmail

Kevin's situation went from worse to worse, drinking more and more, and spending more and more time with Janet. He'd become as addicted to her, and the curves of her body and her sexual talents, as he was to drink. On one unfortunate occasion, when she was naked and in his arms, a blackman barged into their room, almost breaking the door down. Finding them as they were, he went mad and took out a gun, began yelling and swearing, bug-eyed with rage. Kevin was terrified out of his mind but Janet seemed only to be feigning fear as the intruder said at the top of his voice, "That's my lady your with!" This was followed by, "I'm gonna to blow your head off you stinkin drunk. Prepare to meet your maker!"

He was moving around in the room like a raging bull while Janet tried to cover herself with her nightdress, which was designed to cover hardly anything.

The man was huge, and that was putting it mildly. As tall as a tree with a deep, gravelly voice, dishevelled in the way he was dressed. As for poor Kevin, given his pedigree and esteemed upbringing, all he cared about was the scandal. "Please calm down," he said nervously. "What can I do to make you change your mind?"

"You're head on platter," the man replied hoarsely. "White boy," he added.

"Please, don't do anything rash," Kevin went on. "I've clearly hurt your pride. But it's nothing that can't be fixed. So, what will it be?"

"How?" the man hissed. Then, looking him over, "You a *rich* white boy?"

"Yes. And I can give you *anything* you want," Kevin replied.

Kevin realised now that he was being blackmailed and that this was a setup as the man said, "Okay, write me a check for ten thousand dollars or you're both dead meat!" He paused, then eyed Kevin, added, "Come on, write!!"

He got up, desperately trying to cover his private parts with anything he could lay his hands on, and picked his checkbook out of the back pocket of his trousers, all of which occurred while the man pressed his gun to the back of Kevin's head. Kevin scribbled away and the man snatched the slip of paper from Kevin's hands, in a swift move that indicated that he had done this more than once. He left the room, trailing Janet behind him, only to say, "Thanks, sucker!"

Kevin, after collecting himself, called his friend Ray and told him to come and pick him up at this address. He didn't explain why but he wanted him to get here as soon as humanly possible.

Ray climbed up the steps to find Kevin shivering all over, clothes hastily put on, ready to faint. Kevin ambled down the stairs, trying to remain composed, with all the drunks in the bar looking on. Soon after that they were in Broadway, heading to Kevin's home. He got there one after midnight, opening the door gently, with Ray's help, who had to drag him up the stairs so he didn't pitch over, and then dump him in the bed. Ray excused himself after that and promptly left in his car.

The morning sunlight crept in through the multicoloured glass of his bedroom, finally rousing him from his slumber at around 11am. It was like the dead coming back to life, his head throbbing, but all he did when he finally got up was to drink some more. Then he sobbed out load, remembering Sarah, remembering what had just happened to him last night, making him drink some more, till his mother entered his room. She could see what was happening to him, the bags under his eyes, the look of hopelessness on his once youthful face and his slurred speech. None of it was the son that she knew, a man extracted from the bloodline of the Meirs.

Catherine couldn't bear what was going on, what she could see happening to her boy with her own two eyes. She'd also found out about what happened with Sarah. "Kevin, you can't keep living this way."

"Leave me alone," was all Kevin could say, sobbing once again. "This is all your fault."

"What could you possibly mean…"

"You brought me up this way. To hate anybody beneath me. To hate *them*."

"And what does that have to do with Sarah," she asked in all innocence.

He explained exactly what he meant, the drink loosening his tongue. His voice could make anything cry out of pity.

She cried herself, then said, "Forgot her. There's no shortage of girls out there, and from our friends. Girls from good neighbourhoods."

"That's enough," Kevin said in a start. "I *love* Sarah. I love her, I tell you."

He was grabbing onto the glass for sheer life, his lips covered in sweat and tears. Catherine knew that this could be the end of her son and she simply had to do something. She made her decision and left his room, walking down the steps of the stairwell with a determined gait.

She'd taken his mobile phone with her, she found it laying on a chair in his room, and called Jessica straight away. She first apologised for what Kevin had done to Mike, explaining that he regretted his actions. All he had been think about at the time was what had happened to his mother. Then Catherine told her the state that he was in now, how he was destroying himself, begging her to get Sarah to come back to him and forgive him.

Jessica knew Catherine was speaking as a mother and her own better nature took over. She answered her and said, "Don't worry. Everything will be alright."

Scene 2 – A Mother's Request

Mike was reading a book on the civil war-----------. What he'd just gone through confirmed what ---- had said, which was that the civil war was still going on, it was just that words and ideas had taken the place of bullets and bombs.

Smiling to himself he said, "And sometimes its bullets too, ----!"

That's when he recollected how whites in the north treated fellow white people, from the south. Whispering to himself, he added, "So it isn't the colour of your skin that's the only problem."

All he could think about was the coastline, and the Statue of Liberty beyond.

Montesquieu and Voltaire and Rousseau, the Prophet's of justice and equality, he thought. Then he found himself speaking to the fair lady with the torch of liberty in her hand. "When are you going to speak out against what's going on," he said. "I'm waiting, I'm waiting!"

Looking out the window, seeing the sun set on the waters of the Atlantic beyond the skyscrapers, where the great lady was located. Flecks of snow began to fall from the sky like little starlets falling to earth. He needed Jessica's warm body to lay next to him.

The phone rang, knocking him out of his imaginings. It was Jessica.

"Where are you? I need you?" she said.

He got up and took a car to Jessica's house in Brooklyn. As always, she was waiting for him in the garden. They hugged and she greeted him with a kiss.

"What is it," he asked, worried.

"I just needed to see you this evening," she said simply.

She invited him in. They lay in front of the fireplace while Sarah went to the kitchen to make him some coffee. She greeted him as well, saying how much she missed him.

Mike had eyes only for Jessica. "Is there something you want to tell me?"

"Yes," she said hesitantly. "It's to do with Kevin."

"And what's he got to do with me," he replied quizzically.

She explained what had happened, Catherine's phonecall.

"What are you talking about," Sarah said.

"About Kevin," Jessica said.

"It's over between us. I told you that," Sarah said determinedly.

"Slow down. You don't know what he's done to himself. He's killing himself, slowly. His mother begged me, you hear, begged me. Have mercy."

Mike, speaking as calmly as he could, said, "I don't want to be the cause of any man's downfall. And I won't stand between two who love each other. If it means having to swallow my pride, I'll swallow my pride. What just happened, never happened. I'm okay with that."

As angry and adamant as she was, tears were welling up in Sarah's eyes. She still loved him, and couldn't bear to see what he'd come to.

"Catherine's willing to come to you and beg you herself. Don't let her down," Jessica consoled.

Then Mike spoke. "I need a guarantee."

"Anything," Sarah replied, tears streaming down her cheeks. Instinctively she recollected the cross words that had been exchanged between Mike and Kevin. That's when she asked him, "You spoke like a philosopher, like you were Nelson Mandella. But there's something I don't understand. When you said I'm human too. What did you mean?"

"Sarah, we're all, all of us, human beings. I breathe the same air, my blood is as red as Kevin's. And I love Jessica just like Kevin loves you. How else can I prove that I'm human," he added jovially.

That's when they all broke out in laughter. Mike sipped some now cold coffee.

After things calmed down after that, Jessica went to her mobile to call Catherine.

"Thank heavens," Catherine said, after getting the good news.

Catherine and Jessica exchanged tears, while Mike and Sarah looked on quietly.

Chapter 10

Scene 1 – Memories

I never saw your face, my sweet father, and everything my mother Fran told me about you. You went onboard that giant vessel, carrying tanks and planes and soldiers that left the East Coast headed for Iraq, when we were mere infants at the time. Our memories at the time couldn't get enough of your face. All we had to go on were photos, all we had left of you in the end. My mother placed one on the wall, others in the drawers. Mum had some letters from you too from when you were in Iraq, then she left us as well. There's hardly anything left of both of you, just fragment, but we still need you, and you're still here with us.

These thoughts reeled through Jessica's mind as she made her way to Windsor Terrace in Brooklyn, tears on the edges of her eyes. She always made these recollections when was preparing to clean somebody's house, hoping that the next client wasn't nearly as bad, as dangerous, as the previous one. What could she do? They needed the money. Even after Sarah had finally won a scholarship, it still wasn't enough. There was nothing but this thorny road to walk.

Sarah had offered to work as well, to help Jessica pay off their bills and the remainder of their mortgage, now that she was in her sixth year at medical school, but Jessica, after hours and hours of arguing, would only let her work for a few hours a day in the reception of the cancer ward at New York Hospital.

Scene 2 – Too Long a Wait

Sarah, eventually convinced herself to return to Kevin. Before they finally met she learned that he'd already graduated and had his own dental clinic in Broadway.

His father, sick and feeble as he was, had promised his son his own clinic, as a graduation gift. The promise came true and the clinic was furbished. Kevin wanted his own career, as far away as possible from the companies that populated New York and New Jersey, full of employees loyal to his father.

Kevin, busily getting his clinic into working order, received a call from his mother. She was congratulating him but she also promised him a surprise on the front door of his clinic within a few minutes.

"What?" he asked expectantly.

"Wait and see," Catherine replied before cutting the line joyously.

What could it possibly be, Kevin thought, anxious and wondering.

A knock on the door and he almost lept out of his shoes. He rushed to the door and found it was Sarah, the most beautiful present a man could ask for. Her eyes glittered with happiness to see him again, her lightly freckled nose as cute as ever, her body as shapely and arousing as ever. She was certainly dressed in an arousing way. He couldn't resist and grabbed her and carried her up into the air like a ballerina on the stage. The kisses and hugs followed, with romantic nothings whispered by both into each other's ears. They made up for lost time and only after, much after, did they finally get around to fixing up the clinic for its first prospective patients.

Scene 3 – Surrender

Days extended into years and Sarah approached her own graduation day, trying to squeeze in s many hours of work as she could to help her sister pay for her rising expenses. There were more days left to go for Sarah, then the final examination that would make or break her. No more work in the reception till that eventful day came, and if all went to plan she would be on easy street from that point on, becoming a full-fledged and well paid doctor. And that was just the start of it. Then she would marry Kevin, one of the already well off in society, and move to the island of Manhattan to live it up.

As for Catherine, she'd surrendered to the effect that Sarah, poor girl that she was, on her son. Either that or she'd lose her only son forever. Her effect on him was like magic. He went back to his studies as diligent as ever and was now working, and enjoying himself the rest of the time as was the prerogative of the young.

And so the Queen Bee submitted to her son's desires just as the Queen of England accepted her son Charles' decision to marry a girl called Diana, from the common folk of England, technically speaking.

She had enough to take up her time as it was to interfere in her son's life. She was managing her husband's financial empire. Kevin's father had wanted his son to manage it all but the boy had refused to head off to business school. He had a stubborn streak in him. There was no doubting it. And so Catherine had compromised just as she was now. Life went on, and so did her husband's businesses.

Scene 4 – An Angel in Human Guise

Sarah was now conducting her final examination while Jessica stopped cleaning other people's homes, focusing on helping her sister with her studies and working in the restaurant only.

On one occasion, while Sarah was revising and her sister preparing a meal and cups of coffee, Sarah thought to herself, "How can she do it? She's an angel in human guise." It was then that she heard a voice, in the distance, that sounded like Fran: "Jessica *is* an angel!"

That's when Sarah heard the pounding of her own racing heart. It took her quite some time to calm down again. She found her sister sitting next to her, sipping her own cup of coffee while casually leafing through a magazine. As gorgeous as she was as a woman, she really was an angel, thought Sarah. It was like witnessing the Madonna in front of you, in the flesh. She felt like a lightning bolt had passed through her own flesh.

Her, a medical student, believing in angels and ghosts!

Scene 5 – True to Her Word
John Meir was journeying through the reel of his memories as he lay in bed, recollecting when he was a young man, healthy and handsome. He remembered when he took over his own father's businesses.

He remembered his first secretary, Liz, a platinum blonde with crimson lips and a scented body that could slice its way into any man's heart. The miniskirt helped too, exposing her shapely calves and the curve of her thighs and her too frequent entrances into his office, making sure to accidentally drop papers onto the floor to pick them up again. What could he do but succumb to her allure and his conceitedness!

John remembered it all. Wracked with pain that he was, it was like staring at a blank wall that turned itself into a projector screen, displayed all his adventures with Liz in his belated youth. Every single rendevouz, like when she leaned next to him to help him soke up the smell of her perfumes, or let her hair fall loose so it grazed his skin with its softness, or the echo of her high heels on the harsh grounds of the company corridor. She was, in every meaning of the word, a femme fatale. No unlike the Hollywood temptresses that only acted the part. She was the real thing.

It was around that point in his chain of recollections that Catherine entered his room to give him the good news about Kevin and Sarah and how their only son was about to get married.

Sarah finally completed her exams and, one month later, the results were announced and she was first in her class!

Jessica was even happier than her sister. As soon she got the good news she embraced Sarah. It all came to bear, everything they had been through, the good and the bad, weighing down on them at that tear-filled moment.

Cotton buds fell from the wintery sky, showering the city in white as the graduation ceremony began. It was like the whole world was celebrating. Everyone was there. Kevin, Sandy, Mike, Ray, and not just Jessica. They all watched in awe as Sarah rose to the podium to take her hard-won certificate. No sooner had she climbed up the steps that the audience broke out in clapping. She took the certificate and climbed down the steps, from the other side of the platform, cradling the certificate, with hugs and kisses following from family and friends. She gestured to Kevin, knowingly, and he forced himself to shake Mike's hand, swallowing his own pride on this happy occasion. He forced a smile that was not reflective of his true nature on the inside, while Jessica, tears filling her eyes, sat herself next to Mike once more, her alabaster face wavering between smiles and a state of shock.

Sarah was exhausted by the events of that happy day. It was too much for her. The occasion, the hugs and kisses and speeches and partying and well wishing and the applause and the noises ricocheting off the walls of the jam-packed hall. People began to depart at long last and Sarah prepared herself to leave as well, only for Jessica to announce that there was still one more personto meet.

"Please, Jessica. I can't. I'm too tired," Sarah protested. "I just want to go home."

"If you knew who it was, you'd stay!" Jessica replied.

"Who do you mean," Sarah asked.

"It's our mother, Fran," Jessica explain

They both broke out in tears and only after they calmed down did they take a car to holy cross cemetery, remaining quiet the whole time. They bought flowers from a close by flower shop before going in. Jessica's eyes fell on an arrangement of yellow daffodils, leading to another explosion of tears, since those were Fran's favourite flowers.

They walked quickly to their mother's grave, as if they were going to meet her for real, only to slow down once they arrived, step by step.

While placing the flowers on the grave they saw a butterfly flying gently round Fran's gravestone. Its' wings were yellow with black spots, making its way to Jessica's hand and then flying to Sarah and back to Jessica, as if playing with them.

"It's Fran. Her soul," Sarah finally said. "See, she's still with us."

"I wish I could hear your voice, mother," Jessica said after some time had passed between them, in silence. "But I'm sure you can hear me."

Jessica paused before continuing. "Sarah graduated, just like I promised. I took care of her, was her mother and sister and friend and now she's a doctor. I know you were with us the whole time. You could feel what I was going through, but it was all worth it, for Sarah.

"Now I know what you went through for us. Rest easy now, mum. We've made you proud."

Jessica almost collapsed, if it wasn't for Sarah helping her up.

More conversations followed, recounting their mother's many sacrifices for them, after their father had died. Meanwhile, the butterfly continued to float around them.

They were surrounded by gravestones and trees, a quietude exuded from the place. Once they were finished they made their way to the entrance of the cemetery with its marble decorations. Jessica turned one last time to look at where her mother was buried before leaving the place with her sister.

Chapter 11
Scene 1 – Uncle Robert

There was a person who had receded in Jessica's memory, not having seen him since Fran's departure. She made her decision to visit him, after the end of her work day, without telling anybody. She took a cab to where he resided at the very end of Flatbush Avenue. Her mother's face came back into view, as did the man she was headed to, making her all the more determined to bring him back into her life. She reached his house, one of those old, old houses in Brooklyn and Park Slope---, with its attractive brown front and shiny glass windows decorated with white panelling. On closer inspection, after exiting the car and knocking on the front door, she found that the place was not in as good condition as it should be. When the door opened she found that the occupant wasn't in as good condition as he should be either. The grey at his temples had extended to cover all his hair now.----- The buttons on his shirt were not aligned right, button to the appropriate button ole, and his shirt was not tucked in to begin with. The man had a glass of red wine in his hands and his eyes were bloodshot, his face was unshaven and his lips cracked.

The rays of light from the sun attacked his eyes like spears from the sky as he stood uncertainly on his front porch. Even in his stupor, he recognised his visitor and promptly said, "Fran! You've come back to me. Come in, come in!"

Jessica shed a tear for the pitiful state he was in. Weakly she said, "I'm not Fran, uncle Robert."

Bleary eyed, he started at her over and over again to try and wake up out of his drugged state of mind, followed by a whisper, "Jess… ica? Aha…. Jessica!"

"Yes, it's Jessica, uncle Robert. How are you?"

"Like you can see! Please, come in," he replied.

He turned to go inside, slumbering in his footsteps, eventually throwing himself down on a comfy coach, right behind a table covered in empty bottles of liquor and ashtrays loaded with cigarette stubs. Jessica sat on a chair opposite him, listening to his stammering while she tried to see him clearly in the gloom. The room stank of the acrid smell of smoke. The man she saw astride her was someone who had a problem with living. He lived in his broken memories, tearful and with no sense of time, one day like the next, day indistinguishable from night. She could see, feel, how much he'd suffered since Fran had left a man with nothing to keep him company save a bottle.

He had another drink and another puff off from a cigarette that had been waiting for him there, plumes of smoke rising above him, blurring his vision further.

"How have you been doing," she asked in an attempt at conversation.

"I haven't got anything, anyone, to live for" he explained simply.

"Not true," she threw back at him. "There's people worth living for."

"Like who?" he asked.

"Me. And Sarah. You've forgotten us. We need you. Sarah's getting married soon, and who else is going is hand her to the groom?" He was the closest thing they had to a father.
Her words fell on him like early morning dew drops saving plants on the verge of dying from thirst. The blood finally began to course through his veins on hearing those words.
"Get up and fix yourself up, uncle Robert," Jessica said enthusiastically. She got up herself and began to set his house in order. Just letting some light into the house would do the trick. He'd become too accustomed to the dark.
He emptied his glass and stubbed out his cigarette.

Scene 2 – Wedding Gift
The following day, 7am sharp, someone knocked on the door as the chimes of the clock rang out. It was Mike, and his hands weren't empty. He had a charming Pandora bracelet with him, inscribed to Sarah, with a 'J' initial.
"This is my gift to you, dear Sarah," he said.
Pleasant sounds emanated from the house within as Jessica played the piano next to the archaic fireplace, above which was a portrait of Fran, with her husband Jack, in his uniform.

Mere seconds passed before another knock was heard at the door. It was Robert, and in tip top shape. She only recovered after he'd greeted her, with kisses in her cheeks. "Uncle Robert?... Uncle Robert! I can't believe it. It's really you. You're back!"

Jessica finally rose and embrace Mike and Robert while Sarah went off to prepare drinks for this happy occasion.

Scene 3 – Angel Face

The days passed and Kevin grew increasingly impatient. Everything was ready for the wedding, he'd seen to it personally, only the church ceremony and the marriage contract were outstanding. He'd got the contract ready in October. Jessica and Sarah then contacted uncle Robert and told him to be ready for tomorrow, the wedding ceremony would commence at the church of the Holy Trinity in Broadway, informing them that he had to be there early in the morning.

Robert was breathing in life once more, feeling younger than ever now that he had a purpose in life.

The first days of Autumn were evident in the October air. Kevin got into his car, making his way to Flatbush Avenue in Brooklyn, to pick Sarah up. Everybody was as ready as could be for this eventful day, all heading to the church. There was hardly anywhere to sit once the ceremony got going. The priest rose to the alter, waiting for the bride and groom. Robert did the honours, taking Sarah down the aisle in her angelic dress, hand in hand, giving her to Kevin in between smiles and tears. The formal ceremony began and the priest made the announcement, only for Kevin and Sarah to meld into each other with a hot, wet kiss that lasted long enough for the guests to clap and whoop.

The young couple then departed, making their way to Kevin's mansion, by foot, given that it was not so far away from the church. Exiting the church of the holy cross, they were greeted with bells from the larger, grander church of Saint Paul's, congratulating the two of them.

Scene 4 – The Long-Awaited Wedding

The garden at the Meir residence was ready for the young couple, the lights turning on as the sun departed from the sky after the formal occasion at the church. The mansion appeared as if it was encased in pearls, with a pair of angels at the centre of the display case. The only thing missing, Jessica reminisced as she looked on, was Mike. She knew beforehand that he wasn't coming. Her colleagues from work actually asked her where Mike was. She remained silent, eyes glazed over with tears, trying to distract herself with how happy her sister was.

Sarah met her sister's eyes and saw the sadness in them. They communicated through their looks while Kevin had eyes only for his father, in his wheelchair. Standing next to him was Catherine, both relishing the happiness of their only son. The guests, in the meantime, enjoyed themselves, filling the mansion with their noises as they spoke and cheered and clicked and clanged plates and glasses, with the music playing in the background.

The next day came as the last vestiges of the party petered out. A new day in October that began with a pleasant surprise, two tickets to Hawaii for their honeymoon, the land of scantily clad hula dancers dressed in their palm skirts like decorated jewels.

The plane left New York to Hawaii 10am sharp the following morning. They'd be descending into a dense jungle of lovely girls, ushering in Sarah's departure from her old life of hardship to the lap of luxury. They floated into a cave on their love tour and enjoyed themselves in there, among all the other pleasure centres in an exotic vacation spot like Hawaii.

Everything was going fine for them, in the splendour of their exile, on the island of forbidden delights, on the first two days that is. Then the third day came with its own surprises as Kevin's mobile phone exploded into life early in the morning before he had a chance to finish kissing his newly found wife.

It was his mother.

He spoke rapidly on the phone, worried.

His father had just died.

He wasn't surprised. He'd been ill for so long. But the moment of truth still came as a shock.

They packed their bags to make their way back to New York immediately, saddened both by the tragic death of Kevin's father and also by their aborted honeymoon.

Scene 5 – John Meir's Death

The passing of the late John Meir was news, across the country. Everyone knew who he was, and not just his family, friends, employees and business partners, and all made their way to Saint Paul's to pay their last respects.

Kevin returned, with his bride, to find his father in a casket in his bedroom, his wife Catherine standing next to him, crying. He embraced her, crying himself, and the funeral proceedings began. He was later buried at the family burial plot in New York.

The moment of the burial was the hardest. Kevin and his mother, Sarah and, Jessica and Sandy and Ray all their with him and his mother, along with clients and family friends and… two strangers he did not know who were eyeballing him uncomfortably. A young man, about his age, and an older woman that was still quite good looking. He ignored them. He had enough on his plate as it was. Only for his eyes to stumble onto two other people there whom he *did* recognise and who were looking at him with murderous intent.

Scene 6 – Blackmail and Disappointment

The said couple had slipped him a piece of paper at the end of the occasion. Reading it now Kevin knew he was in trouble. It had been Janet and her so-called husband. They wanted $100,000, the blunt message was accompanied with Janet's phone number and the time and place of the handover. Dazed and confused, the only thing he could think of was to call Ray, someone who had gotten him out of more than one fix. He invited him to the clinic, after the work day was over, and true to form Ray showed up on time. Kevin snatched out the piece of paper in a nervous panic and handed it over to his friend only for Ray to say, "Calm down and just tell me what happened."

"You know what happened with Janet, and her... pimp."

"Yes I do," came the simple reply.

"I *saw* them, at the funeral. They want me to pay them to stay quiet. Janet actually put this in my hand!" Kevin begged.

"If you do what they want, they'll be no end to it," Ray replied.

"Then what should I do!"

Ray, measuring his words, said, "Tell Sarah everything. Say, that what happened was when you were drunk, after you two broke up. You weren't aware of what you were doing. That's when Janet took advantage of you. That's a good enough justification as any, and I'm sure Sarah will forgive you. She knows you're flawed, like all of us are."

Ray won Kevin over with his logic. It would be risky but, in all honesty, what else could he do?

By 11pm Kevin was back home with all of the weight of the world on his shoulders. Sarah, as usual, greeted him with passionate kisses and her semi-translucent clothes, only to find in his features a man whose mind was clearly elsewhere. Where was his usual smile?

"What's wrong Kevin" she finally said.

He was too anxious to be coherent, the words struggling to dislodge themselves off the tip of his tongue. He had to muster all his strength to tell her exactly what had happened. With all his apologies he'd nonetheless hurt her, her pride, as he said: "What could I do, Sarah, after you dumped me? I was trying to forget you with all the drink and that's when that… whore took advantage of me."

Sarah knew the kind of predicament Kevin had found himself in and she found it in herself to forgive him. "I'll be with you, when you meet her."

Kevin finally breathed a sigh of relief, relaxing his crisis ridden features.

They didn't do anything that night, sleeping uneasily as they waited for the sun to rise and the eventual meeting to take place. Sarah, true to her word, had 'prepared' before heading off to bed.

The dawn light crept its way in through the stained glass windows of Kevin's mansion. The young couple got up, Kevin knowing he wasn't headed to his clinic that day. Instead he remained indoors, Sarah by his side and a suitcase by her side, till the clock struck an appropriate time. They left, rendezvousing with Ray first, and then heading off to confront Janet and her man.

It didn't take them too long to get there. They found Janet and her 'husband' waiting expectantly at designated location they had chosen, out in the open. Kevin and Ray made their way cautiously to them, Kevin with the suitcase in his hand, while Sarah took her time.

Janet extended her hand to snatch the suitcase. She opened it in a hurry only to find it empty!

"You makin fun of us whiteboy," her husband said. It turned out his name was Steve.

"You're playing with fire," Janet said for her part. "I've got it all down on tape!"

That's when Sarah walked up to them, with a slow pace.

"And who are you," Janet asked.

"I'm Kevin's wife," Sarah said proudly.

That took the wind out of her sails, her and her husband. They'd bet everything on the humiliation, that Kevin was terrified his sweetheart would find out. They'd been betting on John Meir first, then he had to die on them.

"I'll show the world what you husband is like," Janet hissed back.

"Do what you want," Sarah replied. "And remember to send me a personal copy while you're at it."

While the dialogue was intensifying, a police car slowed down next to where Kevin's car was parked. The blood in Janet's veins froze, along with Steve's blood as well. They thought that Kevin had set a trap for them.

They made a run for it, while Kevin and Sarah and Ray just stood there; quiet while jubilant on the inside.

"Fate dealt the last blow," Sarah finally said.

The three of them looked up and above at the sky as the sun shone on, breaking through the clouds for one glorious moment of grace.

Chapter 12

Scene 1 – A State of Calm

The streets were almost vacant. Only the odd person or vehicle made its presence felt in the suburbs of the city in their slow motions in the roads. Even the shops were inexplicably closed, for a foreigner making his way to the country. If he asked the locals, however, he' find the exact same answer from every respondent. It was Thanksgiving. This was the day when all Americans were the same, coloured by same human brush. No white, no black, the country pulled all of it races together and made Americans out of them, a breed of man who cherished the flag above all else, holding it high n this planet in this universe.

A lonely astronaut from another planet, wherever he chose to land, New York, Manhattan or anywhere for that matter, would be dumbfounded to understand what had happened to all the people.

Only to find a multitude of people pouring into the streets in boisterous carnivals filled with girls and dancers parading around a giant Mickey Mouse balloon that could take on the largest skyscraper. Not to mention the giant balloon Turkey that everybody was planning to consume this said day.

That alien astronaut would find one answer and one answer only to his queries about the peculiar happenings this day, namely, that's it's the first Thursday of November, or Thanksgiving Day, a thoroughly American concoction. All the States in the US of A agreed to eat roast and stuffed turkey with a side order of mashed potatoes and cranberry sauce and pumpkin pie. It's the food that unites Americans, poor and rich alike. What a bewitching celebration!

Scene 2 – Thanksgiving

Mike was spending the occasion with Jessica at her house in Flatbush. Jessica had asked him to move in, especially now that Sarah was no longer there, and not only to keep her company. Their already raging passion took off and reached new heights in the days following Sarah's wedding.

Ideally they all should have been spending Thanksgiving together, Mike and Jessica, Sarah and Kevin, at the Meir mansion, but Mike and Kevin just didn't see eye to eye with each other on so many things they both thought the better of it. Even such a happy occasion as this would not suffice. The Meir residence was more exuberant than usual this time of year, lighting up half of Broadway in the evening, with Kevin's small family celebrating with Sandy and Ray, sitting around the dining table and clinging to pieces of dialogue passing between the host family and the guests in a delicious hubbub of quiet conversation. Catherine was the true hostess of this event and instigator of the conversations.

She began by asking Ray how he was doing and where he worked now.

"In a financial brokers," he replied.

"Why not hire him," Catherine opined.

"I'll take it under consideration," Kevin said unseriously.

"I'd have no objections, for my part," Ray answered happily.

Just as the conversation was warming up, Catherine's phone came to life. Recognising the number, she said with some disquiet, "It's Edward." That was the company lawyer. "What could he want at a time like this?"
Speaking to the caller Catherine said, "Happy Thanksgiving, Edward."
"And the same to you," Edward replied.
"Yes," she said without commenting.
"Nothing at all. I just want you and Kevin to be here tomorrow morning to read the will."
"We'll be there as you wish Edward."

Scene 3 – The Meir Will
Catherine woke up early next morning, forcing herself to get up after yesterday's festivities, heading off to the Meir company with Kevin at the steering wheel, and all to see the company lawyer.

The employees greeted them warmly and Edward exited his office to do the same, after hearing the noise of the well wishers. After greeting them he invited them into his office only to find an attractive middle aged woman and a young man with her.

Kevin and his mother were reluctant to sit down. Seeing this Edward took the initiative and spoke about the will, talking openly about the family secrets in front of these strangers. Where had Catherine seen them before, she wondered? She searched her cluttered, dusty memories of all these years, trying to locate the face to this strangely clam women, and her too short skirt.

"Mr Edward, it seems we've come at a bad time since you clearly have guests," Catherine said in an effort to break the uncomfortable silence.

"Oh, these aren't guests," Edward replied. "This is John jr., Kevin's brother. And this lady is his mother, Liz."

The words fell like bullets onto Catherine's ears. She had to sit herself down, which made her feel like she'd been shoved off the rooftop of Manhattan's tallest building. Meanwhile, Edward serenely took out the last will and testament.

Before he could utter another word, Catherine broke out and said, "What the hell are you talking about Edward? Have you lost your mind? John Meir has only one son, Kevin."

"I'm afraid the will says that John Jr. is his other son. His illegitimate son," Edward explained casually.

"What did you just say? John Jr.?" She placed her head between her hands, stooped over, trying to gather together any semblance of life – her life with her lying, cheating husband who'd tricked her all these long years, in sickness and in health.

She remembered how, when they'd first married, he'd told her he wanted a boy and to name him John Jr., only to change his mind some years later when Catherine had got pregnant. She'd told him that his wish would now come true, only for him to say that any name would do. Kevin would sound nicer than 'junior', he'd said. She hadn't fathomed why he'd changed his mind at the time, and hadn't bothered to ask why. But now she knew. Liz had beaten her to it!

She journeyed backwards more than twenty years. Liz, it was. His secretary. How John had repeated her name over and over again in the mansion.

Catherine rose her head from the ashes of her desiccated memories and the wounds of the past. "So *you're* Liz," she managed to say.

"Yes, madam," Liz replied.

The blue of Catherine's eyes was steadily turning red, as if her eyes were going to leap out at Liz.

Edward took the will out of its envelope and said, explicitly, that half of everything went to John Jr.

"This can't be," Kevin said weakly.

"I'm afraid it's spelt out here in the last will and testament," Edward said. "There's no avoiding it."

Kevin raged on the inside and it showed in the deadly stare in his eyes. John Jr., however, didn't rage back. All that was evident on his face was a deep loneliness, a boy who had been orphaned in more than one way. Catherine fell into a stone cold silence after that while the lawyer busied himself with more legal details.

Liz, on the inside, was ecstatic, with the tremendous inheritance that was being passed over but she made sure not to show it. She could see the tension in Kevin and in his mother. Instead she explained that she didn't know anything about the will and that it was Edward who contacted her, all the way in California, where she'd gone to raise John Jr. out of wedlock. His father had been spending on him the whole time.

Liz said it all with supreme femininity, with her heavy Brooklyn accent.

Catherine was quaking under the strain of it all. She knew precisely just how much her late husband owned. She just couldn't accept that these two were going to get half of it, all in one go. but it was the law. What could she do?

As if that wasn't bad enough, when the meeting was finally over and Kevin and his mother left the company, they found the press waiting for them.

The late John Meir was a celebrity in his own right and many an industrious journalist had been able to find out what was going to happen today, before ether Kevin or Catherine did. And Liz and John Jr. were there to field questions as well on the marbled entrance to the company headquarters.

A veritable wall of people lay ahead of the exiting parties. One journalist, a lady, was able to get a question in to Kevin: "What does it feel like know that you know that you have a brother?"

"First of all," Kevin snapped. "That's just a claim. We'll see what the truth is afterwards."

As for John Jr. he had something very different to say. "All my life I wanted to have a brother. Wanted to have a normal family like everybody else. To have a father there with us. I only ever saw him when he could make it to where we lived. Felt like I was an orphan growing up. And when I turned twenty I felt like an exile, like I'd committed a crime. Like any of it was my fault."

Chapter 13

Scene 1 – A Thunderbolt
"Illegitimate son of John Meir emerges after 20 year absence", that was the main headline plastered onto the front page of many a major newspaper, and quite a few magazines as well. Other headlines included "Kevin denies John Jr. is his brother and accuses the mother of fraud", "What will happen to the inheritance", "Illegitimate son earns the sympathy of the public and the media", and so on and so forth. Kevin was in the limelight now, whether he liked it or not, as if he didn't have enough to worry about on his plate. He was fuming on the inside and the mere glance at a newspaper containing those headlines would drive him overboard!

Everyday, when he'd get the morning paper, he'd see one of these headlines and he'd lose control and start smashing things, forcing Sarah into a panicky wakefulness. She'd spend the rest of the morning trying to calm him down, to no avail, witnessing him tear up the papers in a murderous rage.

On one occasion she had to confront him and say, "Why are you so angry? The will was clear, John Jr. is your brother. It's a fact. I can't believe how this has changed you." He wasn't the Kevin she'd fallen in love with. Finally she added, "You have to do the noble thing."

He was drenched in sweat. The ordeal was bearing down on him, physically. He lurched down on the nearest coach and held his head between his hands. Then and only then did his breathing calm down. It was all slipping through his fingers, his father's inheritance, all that hard work going to these undeserving... strangers. Sarah found that she had no choice but to give him the good news, a little ahead of schedule, the only antidote to his gloomy mood.

"I'm pregnant," she said in a gentle, seductive voice.

"What," he said, stupefied. It took all his remaining strength to pull his head up so he could face Sarah.

Smiling, she repeated, "I'm pregnant!"

He gave her a neutral expression, his face moving swiftly from one reaction to the opposite reaction. The smile that eventually spread over his features seemed maniacal. Then he got up in a start and took her in his hands, lifting her up into the air like she was a butterfly.

That's when Catherine saw them. "What is it children, please tell me?!"

"Sarah's pregnant, mum!" Kevin said gleefully at the top of his voice.

"Pregnant!" she could hardly believe it herself. "Since when," Catherine asked Sarah like she was her daughter.

"From about a month," Sarah replied. "I found out it was a boy just yesterday. He's Adam, the boy I've always wanted!"

Kevin and his mother were a bit too shocked to reply straight away, noting Sarah's choice of name, but Kevin said nonetheless, "Anything you want, my dear Sarah. Adam it is!"

The thrill of the good news had erased the memories of the reading of the will and everything seemed to be back to normal, till Catherine asked, "But what are we going to do about Liz and John?"

She put out the sorcery of the moment with that query, bringing her son back to square one. Sarah moved quietly away from them to wallow by herself. They almost didn't notice as Sarah prepared for herself for the day she would give birth, but still Catherine's angry words would pursue her unabated.

"I've heard that John Jr. keeps showing up at the company and has even got his own office. He's a partner in the firm," Catherine's screechy voice went on and on, invading Sarah's beleaguered mind. "Kevin, you've got to forget your clinic, at least for now. You've got to be at the company, to make sure he doesn't take over and cut us out of everything."

Kevin had no choice but to go along, or else everything would slip through his hands.

From that point onwards he spent less and less time in his clinic and more and more time at his father's company. It didn't take long to find out that John Jr. knew a thing or two about business and that meant Kevin was at a disadvantage.

He would also appoint Ray in the accounting department, as his mother suggested. What choice did he have? It was either that or lose the company. He was in shifting sands and he knew it. His life as it had originally been laid out was no more. He had to go with the flow or sink.

Scene 2 – Racism Pursues Mike

The sky was grim that night, with only a few tentative stars in evidence, the curtain of the night draping the windows in its gloom. Sarah let Catherine and Kevin plot and scheme to their heart's content. Her mind was elsewhere. She made her way to the phone and told Jessica how she was pregnant and then made it back to her bedroom to rest from the ordeal of the day.

The news reached the friends and relatives in the Meir family quickly enough and they descended on them in no time at all to congratulate them and bring gifts in preparation for the day young Adam would come on the scene. Sarah saved up all the presents and placed in them in a specially designed baby room, full of baby clothes and teddy bears and toys and oversized pictures of children smiling and playing, and warm words of welcome. As luck would have it Jessica had a holiday in order as it was so she spent an especially long time decorating the room with Sarah.

The two sisters were oblivious to the machinations going on around them in the Meir residence. As far as they were concerned this was the beginning of the end of all the sorrows they'd endured in their life, with their father then their mother passing away.

"How's the pregnancy," Jessica volunteered.

"The doctor says it isn't stable," Sarah replied. "My uterus is enlarged. He's prescribed some medication."

"What," Jessica said, stunned at hearing those words. "How can you let yourself work when the pregnancy is at risk? You've got to stay home and rest as much as you can."

She doodled on her for some time more, cautioning her against exerting herself, for her sake and the baby's sake, then excused herself to head back to Flatbush and to Mike.

Sarah asked her to relay her greetings to him, thanking him for making her elder sister so happy.

Jessica made it back home and spent the evening in Mike's arms, all the way into the early morning. They promptly got up, went through their daily routine, and headed off to their work at the restaurant.

Mike could barely keep up with the number of guests that day, greeting them and showing them to their tables, while Jessica was in the kitchen preparing the meals. That's when a tall, dignified and attractive woman made her way into the restaurant, carrying a baby with her.

Mike showed her to her table and took some time to tease the baby and make him feel at home, only for the lady to whisk the child away from him in a sudden move. He swallowed his smile and asked the new guest what she would like.

"Nothing at all," she said from off the tip of her nose. That's when her eyes fell on another waiter there, who was white, and gave him the order instead. The whole time she was being served, she looked at him from the corner of her eye, with disdain.

Mike retreated into the background, his heart weighing down on him, threatening to break his ribcage in two.

It brought back more bad memories. He's been walking the streets once only to see an old man, a black man, dishevelled and grim, asking passersby if they had seen his lost daughter. The man had to sit down on the pavement. His feet were sore from all his wonderings, and nobody would give him the time of day, till a fat white man finally spoke to him, telling him to get lost.

The look of abject terror in the old man's eyes, glowing like stars, still lay with Mike. Why? Why did people do such things? All the pains of his people, from the time they first left the coast of Africa, in chains, to this very day were contained in that one question, in that one incident Mike had witnessed.

But what could he do? In the end he put on another smile and resumed his work duties, greeting other guests into the restaurant. But Jessica knew there was something wrong, when he went to the kitchen later in the day. She could see it in the slump of his shoulders. The tears were battling in his eyes to get out.

She had to know what happened. He didn't answer, but said he would leave work early today and tell her what happened when they were at home.

Scene 3 – Pregnancy at Risk

The doctor had warned Sarah and how the slightest move could lead to an abortion, and Kevin made arrangements, hiring two nurses to look after her, one on the night shift and one in the daytime. On one particular night one of the nurses came late for her shift at 6pm and Sarah had to get up by herself to head to the bathroom. She became dizzy and tried to balance herself, placing her hand on the wall, falling instead. She began to bleed terribly, screaming out to the maid, "Rita, Rita!"

Rita ran out of the kitchen where she'd been, Catherine behind her. She saw what was happening and called an ambulance immediately, while Catherine looked on in shock, not knowing what to do.

Mere minutes passed and the ambulance came to carry her off to the hospital. At that exact same moment Kevin was in his company, with Ray, only for his phone to ring. It was his mother.

"Sarah's in the hospital. You've got to get here, right now!"

Not long after Kevin and Ray were in the hospital, only to find Sarah in the operating room. The doctor came out and regretted to inform them that Sarah had lost the baby. Kevin couldn't believe what he'd heard at first. He was so shocked he didn't know what to feel. Then his sorrow turned to anger. He burst into the operating room and yelled at his wife, "Why, Sarah? Didn't we tell you to be careful!"

Sarah hadn't even recovered. She wasn't half aware of what was going on around her. She couldn't see Kevin clearly. Her eyes were too full of tears over what had happened to her baby. Kevin, uncomprehending of this, burst out of the room as quickly as he'd entered, furious. He met the doctor on the way out. The man explained, insisted, that this was inevitable. The pregnancy was just too unstable. He also explained that pregnancy in the future would be even more difficult, after the loss of this baby.

Kevin, angry as before, slouched his back onto the wall, defeated.

Scene 4 – Sarah Returns Home

Shortly after, once Sarah was sufficiently recovered, she returned to the Meir mansion. She wasn't fully recovered, of course. It still hurt too much, the pain of losing her baby and the physical scars of the ordeal. Her eyes were glazed over and as soon as she entered the house, she went to the baby room. She was shivering all over as her hand grazed over the walls with the pictures of happy children, her eyes scanning the toys and games she'd prepared for Adam. Catherine walked up behind her and bombarded her with her bitter voice. Sarah, as if deaf, ignored her and moved into the room, hugging the toys she'd bought for her infant son. She could almost see him, Adam, playing with them. If was like a ghost was in the room with her. She had eyes only for him. She could only hear his voice. She finally spoke, "Why did you leave me?"

She wished she had seen him, once would have been enough, to say goodbye.

Rita was passing by the room at that moment and heard Sarah's subdued words, words that drove her to tears. She forced herself to go into the room. She could see Sarah, losing her balance, abut to topple over. She grabbed her just in time. Later she took her, almost guided her, to the bedroom where she lay down on her bed, surrendering to an uneasy sleep.

Chapter 14

Scene 1 – Depression and Apathy

Vodka was her companion over the dark days after Sarah had lost her infant child. Catherine took every opportunity to remind her, to express her sense of disappointment, becoming the classical mother in-law. Even Kevin chipped in from time to time. Sarah couldn't resume her work at the hospital, burying herself in her sorrows. She couldn't abide to look at Catherine. Just the sight of her made her feel like she was looking at something vampiric and not of this world.

The more she drank, the more the world she lived in wasn't real. She saw things and heard things that weren't there, the mansion turning into a ghostly residence where children talked and played and ran and then disappeared without trace. One particular day she drank so much she fell unconscious, falling onto the ground in a deep sleep, her knees pulled up into her stomach. That's when her mother, Fran, appeared to her.

She descended on her like an angel from high and above, cradling a child in her arms. A black child.

"This is Adam," Fran said with her ethereal voice.

When Sarah protested that that could not be her Adam, her mother insisted that it was Adam.

"Take care of him," Fran whispered. The child smiled towards Sarah, melting her heart.

She moved towards him, stretching out her arms to embrace him…

That's when she came too. But she heard mother in her waking state as well.

"Come back to yourself.

Sarah looked around her. Could it have been real, she wondered.

She had someone in the world, even after all she'd been through. Fran was still there, looking over her. She remembered how Fran sang to her when she was a little girl, before going to bed.

It did the trick, helping her sleep at night in peace without having to resort to the bottle.

Scene 2 – Jessica's Pregnancy

Jessica was on her way to Broadway, to the Meir mansion, to check on her sister. Her eyes caught someone in the background, someone who looked like a burglar, a black man, but her mind was elsewhere. She ignored him and made her way to the mansion. Meeting her sister, she could see how much she'd been through. Rings under her eyes, a pale sickly hue to her skin, body turning flabby.

She held her hand and said, "Come back to yourself Sarah, there's still so much to live for."

"What could be worth living for," Sarah said weakly.

"Yes, there is," Jessica underlined. "Love. Hope. The days you still have in your life."

"You'd don't know anything, sis," Sarah replied.

That's when she told her how Catherine was mistreating her, and the fight between Kevin and John Jr., and the bad dreams and waking dreams she'd been suffering.

"It's all because of the drink," she consoled her. "Stop drinking and it'll all go away. And your strong enough to handle the rest of it."

Jessica then filled her in on the remaining details of her life. Mike was heading off to Ohio to meet his family. His parents were buried there but he still some family there. And then she gave her little sister the big surprise.

"What is it," Sarah said expectantly. "Anything at all. Anything that'll make me happy!"

"I'm pregnant," Jessica said, beaming.

It came as a pleasant shock to Sarah. Was it a coincidence, she wondered, just before Jessica said, "I'll bring you your Adam, the boy you always wanted!"

The words were like magic for Sarah. "Does Mike know?" she asked.

"No. I want to tell him till he gets back from Ohio."

The two sisters spent a long time together that day, and it was only when Jessica was satisfied that Sarah was well recovered enough that she decided to leave. She spent some time at intersection on 79 River Side, window shopping, till she hailed a cab to head back home.

Scene 3 – Mike's Hometown

A plane hung in the air, heading from New York to Ohio, and Mike was onboard it. He hadn't forgotten home after all these years in the big apple. He hadn't forgotten his parents, who were buried in a graveyard next to West Branch Lake----CHECK---- in one of rural towns of Ohio, where he'd spent some of the best years of his life. The town was populated with farmers and wage labourers and people headed to the city to find work.

It was here that Mike had cut his teeth, as a man. His first love was Francesca, a Mexican girl that worked at the local bar. She was four years his senior. He was only 15 at the time, a young stud on the rise. He didn't even have to make the first move. It was Francesca who confronted him with many a clandestine rendezvous near the lake, creeping up on him through the forests.

It was the forests that had brought them together. He would chop away on logs for the bar she worked at. He'd been in his jeans, naked from the waist up, gleaming with sweat in the heat of the sun, an open invitation.

She was in her prime herself, with her topless outfit and slender hips and he'd become addicted to her as much as she was addicted to him. The forest was the perfect place to consume their relationship. It wasn't just the privacy and seclusion and the scenery. It was the smell. The smell of the pine needles and flowers was intoxicating. She done it so many times with Mike there in the forest that nothing turned her on like the smell of the place.

On one occasion she's stolen his shirt, the one he left by his side while he chopped away on the logs, or made love to her. Whenever she wanted to remember him, she'd sniff his shirt, and it would drive her into a sexual frenzy, and she'd have to meet him and leap at him no matter the time.

It was only Mike's commitment to his career, to finding a better career for himself, that put an end to their love. He had to leave and she had to cope with it.

It had been twenty years, Mike reminisced to himself.

He landed in Ohio airport and hired a car to head into the countryside back to his hometown. He dropped by his aunt Mary first of all, the eldest of his remaining relatives. But even while there he was drawn inexorably to Andrew's Bar, where Francesca had worked.

Some of the landmarks of the town had changed on the way there, but the bar itself was as it was. Andrew had inherited ot from his grandfather and the place was true to its classical roots, a literal part of the Wild West. He found Andrew behind the counter, with his bushy eyebrows and the hair at his temples, only, and freckles of red all over his very white face. He took up a stool while the barman was pouring some drinks to guests already there.

Andrew, without asking, poured Mike a glass of wine, prompting him to ask, "Don't you remember me? Remember Henry, the carpenter, Mary's brother?"

Andrew shut his eyes for an instant and mouthed some names silently on his lips, tasting for something he couldn't identify. Then his bushy eyebrows rose as he yelled out, "Yes... Yes, I remember. Forgive me my boy, I haven't seen you in a long, long time. You were so young when you was here." He shook his head to clear away more cobwebs then added, "Yeah, I remember you when you brought us wood for the fireplace, with Francesca. Mike... Mike it was. Yeah, Francesca would take her time with you, went to you even when we had plenty for the fireplace!"

"And where is she now," Mike asked. "I don't see her here."

Sighing deeply, Andrew said, "She got married, a while ago. Then God knows where she went with her husband." He paused unexpectedly then added, "She sends me the odd letter, even mentions you once in a while. And your aunt Mary. She even says she may come back, but hasn't so far." He said it like he missed her.

Mike had drained his glass of wine by then and left Andrew to get back to his regulars.

He made his way back to his sweet, old aunt Mary, enjoying the view along the way of the lake in the distance, pinning for the day of his youth when this was the whole of the world for him.

Her house was surrounded by trees and autumn had left its marks on them. Some brown leaves broke from the branches and fell on top of his head.

Scene 4 – Ray Quits

Kevin had given up on his clinic for earnest now, dedicating his life to block John Jr.'s every move, using Ray as he eyes and ears. That being said, John Jr. knew his stuff, a young man with business degrees and a natural acumen for making money and managing people. John Jr. was just as dedicated to the Meir inheritance, having taken half of the company himself in one bold move. Then Kevin tried to sell over some of the company's stocks, and John Jr. blocked him. That was just the first salvo in a never ending chain of decisions and counter decisions.

That's when Ray discovered just how maniacal Kevin was. He was willing to sink the whole company, rather than leave it to John Jr.

At one point Ray snapped and told Kevin that his rash decisions were going to bankrupt the company.

He couldn't believe it. This wasn't the Kevin he knew and trusted. He finally handed in his own resignation, pulling the paper out of his pocket and placing in front of Kevin on his desk before storming out of the room, out of the company premises.

Sandy, Ray's wife, had no idea he'd taken this decision. He called Sarah and Jessica innocently and invited them to her daughter's birthday party. Amanda was just turning four, on Sunday.

Mike had just made it back from Ohio, grabbing hold of Jessica after returning to Flat Bush. She told him about the birthday party they'd been invited to and then whispered into his ear, "I have a surprise for you!"

She proceeded to strip in front of him. When she was completely naked he asked jovially, "Is this my surprise?"

"No, no!" she replied.

"Was that my surprise," Mike responded.

"I won't tell you," Jessica teased. "I'll only tell you on Amanda's birthday, in front of everybody."

That's when Mike apologised, for not being able to go to the birthday party. He didn't want to rub up against Kevin. Jessica was adamant though. It took a great deal of persuading, even in her nude state, but it worked in the end, especially after they lapped up the nectar of lovemaking.

Scene 5 – The Truth about Kevin

And so on Sunday Mike and Jessica took their car to Sandy's house, way at the end of Flatbush Avenue – almost another part of town. The birthday party hadn't begun yet but there was no shortage of people there, bringing gifts with them and presenting them to the lucky little girl. The person conspicuous by his absence was Kevin.

Amanda stood there, by her parents, Ray and Sandy, all giggles and smiles as she was the centre of attention. Later she went to the piano and struck up a tune. As she played away happily, people sipping on their glasses of red and white wine, Kevin made his appearance. He had Sarah with him, naturally, but he took his good time to shake hands with the guests, and also true to form he ignored Mike entirely. Everybody noted this impolite move. Then Kevin made his way to Ray and whispered into his ear: "The administration didn't accept your resignation."

More whispers moved between the two during the festivities till Mike made his way towards them. Directing his words to Kevin with supreme confidence he said, "Are you still they way you always were?"

"That's not really any of your business," Kevin replied.

"You know, I have plenty of white friends," Mike said, recollecting his trip back home. "Things have changed since the olden days. The world keeps changing. That's the way of the world."

"Well, I guess I'm the big exception. I've got no reason to change," Kevin threw back at him.

Ray couldn't believe his ears. He had no idea Kevin could be such a conceited snob.

Jessica was standing a goodly distance away, with Sarah and Sandy and little Amanda, but she could sense what was happening between Mike and Kevin.

With her trademark feminine intuition, and feminine intelligence, she took advantage of a location in the room that was three feet above the ground, stood above it and announced to all who would listen: "Ladies and gentleman. Today I inform you that I am with child, pregnant with *Adam*. I've already chosen his name. For my dearest Sarah's sake!"

Mike drove himself towards her like a madman, dazed with happiness. He lifted her up in his strong arms, like a tree he'd felled, and transformed her into a ballerina. The party was no longer about the little sweetheart Amanda but about Adam and his two prospective parents.

That's when Kevin had had enough and left the party, a gruesome expression pressed on his face.

Chapters 15

Scene 1 - Merciless Memories

John Jr. lived in a flat with his mother, another one of the endless belongings of his late father John Meir. It was located at the intersection of Wall Street and Broadway, nearby the headquarters of the Meir company. With all the wealth they had inherited, however, Liz was still not happy. She was worried about her son. He was lonely. He'd been lonely his whole life, and he refused to do anything about it, such as get married or at least fall in love or have a girlfriend.

She just wanted him to be happy. He was young, he was handsome, he was rich. He had all that was needed to find a girl. And it wouldn't hurt to have a grandson to inherit the Meir wealth as well, she told him to his face.

Every one of Liz's words hurt, all he could do was mumble the usual response that he would find a girl and make her proud, eventually.

Then he excused himself, went to the bathroom and wept silently. He was slouched over, hands on holding him up on the sink, looking at himself in the mirror and the image of defeat and hopeless that lay before him. Caught between anger and sadness, he didn't know what to do.

He knew that as she was saying was right. That's why he couldn't confront her. He left the apartment then, taking his car and travelling between the coastline, the lights of the big city extending their colourful embrace on the waters of the inhospitable sea of the Atlantic.

He got out and walked and walked till he could walk no more. He sat himself down on a rock bench and looked out into the distance, stroking his hair back. Then he began to remember.

Anne. The one and only girl he'd ever been with. Beautiful, sexy Anne. They'd met when he was at business school, a classmate, a beautiful blonde that was drawn to him by his silence and his fortitude of character. It had taken some time but they'd consummated the sexual act, his on time in point of fact, and boy had they let themselves go loose in the youthful frenzy.

It may have been his first time, but it certainly wasn't Anne's. She knew the while rulebook of lovemaking, and how to throw the rules out of the window. You'd never guess it but she was into kinky sex, but she was. She began by laying him down on the bed while she slowly and seductively took her clothes off, like a stripper in a club, taking advantage of his hunger and longing.

Then she teased him with her extremities, forcing him to lap up her body, every part of it, till he couldn't take it anymore and he made love to her, over and over again.

She didn't moan. She *screamed*. She enjoyed screaming, turning pleasure into pain as she rode him. The only thing you could hear other than her screams was her laughter.

After that he removed himself from her life and never allowed himself to get involved in another girl's life, despite his love for Anne and his desire for a woman's body.

He was drowning in his memories now, tears streaming from his eyes.

He finally forced himself up and gathered himself together, what was left of him, and left.

Not long after he went back to work. Despite his personal troubles he was a hard worker and he never neglected his duties at the company. It was his sense of responsibility that drew him to Ray and why he insisted that Ray stay on when he handed in his resignation. He convinced the board of director's to refuse the resignation. When he saw Ray there the following day, he was jubilant, and invited him to have a coffee with him, chatting away about anything other than work. And that's when he *really* got to know him.

Ray, in turn, befriended him, growing to respect him as the company's profile grew and grew over time. This was a far cry from Kevin's performance, which led to a growing distance between the two old friends.

On one occasion Ray came out of John Jr.'s office, with tears in his eyes. He'd entrusted him with his secrets. Ray was a secretive person and didn't tell anybody what went between then, even his wife Sandy. On another occasion Sandy was running an errand and she saw John Jr. coming out of a doctor's clinic. She told Ray about it when she got home. The clinic belonged to a heart doctor.

Ray laughed it off by saying that John Jr. was checking up on his mother who has some heart trouble, and that was all.

Scene 2 – Waiting for Adam

Mike and Jessica, Sandy and Ray, and the Meir family were all drawing closer and closer together. Kevin was the only odd one out. Even so, things got better with time, especially as Jessica's pregnancy progressed. She was now in her eighth month. As the fates would have, on one occasion Sarah and Sandy and Ray were all at her house to congratulate her, only for an unexpected visitor to come – uncle Robert. He added his gift to the ensemble and that's when the occasion really got going, with clicks and clangs of champagne glasses.

Then Ray's phone came to life in his coat pocket. It was John Jr., he announced to Sarah.
"Kevin's brother," she mouthed.
"How are you," Ray said.
"Where are you," came John Jr.'s own question.
"I'm with Mike and Jessica."
"Why not invite him," Mike said to Ray.
Ray nodded and told John Jr. how to get here. As luck would have it he was already on the road in his car, driving over Brooklyn Bridge. He'd be there is no time at all.
Sarah was a bit perturbed about this final meeting, but she kept her reservations to herself. Kevin had badmouthed his brother in front of Sarah, telling her he was a greedy idiot and wanted to destroy everything his father had built.
Shortly afterwards Ray exited the house to meet John Jr. and promptly returned to show him in.

John Jr. was a handsome young man, almost the spitting image of his father John Meir, and quite a gentle individual, someone who didn't like noise and large crowds, soft spoken and whose words always left the right impression on the person he was talking to. He wasn't at all what Sarah expected. He greeted everybody well then made his way to Jessica, congratulated her and gave her a gift that was clearly expensive, and then met with Mike, who took to him immediately. Ray returned with a glass of champagne and the festivities continued as the soft music in the background warmed up.

Sarah continued to observe John Jr., studying his every move with her feminine intuition. She could find any of the character flaws her husband had talked about. Quite contrary, he was a sweet and gentle soul and morally upright, and people took to him despite his shyness, particularly Ray, who was Kevin's confident and very best friend. There was also a deep sadness in him. She could see it in the furtive movements of his eyes, despite his clear happiness at being here with people that he know considered to be his extended family.

Scene 3 – A Newborn

Jessica's screams rose and rose, only for her to fall silent in an instant, and then the cries of a new life as her infant son Adam screamed his first scream. Mike, Sarah, Ray and Sandy were all there to hear it, standing just outside the hospital room, waiting for Adam. The nurse came out and congratulated them, with the stock words they used in these kinds of places – both the mother and the baby are fine – for them to push their way in to the room to see for themselves that Jessica and little Adam were fine. That's when they were greeted with a surprise – his colour.

He was neither fully African or fully Caucasian. He had dark skin, like his father no doubt, but his mother's green eyes.

His hair wasn't African either, and his face was hard to pin down. It was his first day in life, in all cases.

Mike remained by Jessica's side, stroking her blonde hair gently. He'd secretly been hoping the boy would look like his mother, to spare him a little of what'd he'd had to go through, but the love in Jessica eyes made him forget everything and just be thankful that they had a baby of their own.

The days came and went and at an accelerating pace and a whole year passed since Adam's entry into the world. He was growing up to be a handsome boy. Everybody was enamoured with him, especially Sarah, who couldn't stand to be away from him. She invited Jessica to bring him over with her for dinner on one occasion, but Jessica had to decline the invitation. She had been at work at the restaurant and got a call from the babysitter telling her that Adam was suffering from a fever and that it was getting worse. Jessica left the restaurant in a rush to find Adam in his crib, crying and crying. She called Mike to say she was taking the baby to see the doctor.

"What is it?" What's going on," he asked, worried.

"His temperature is rising."

"Wait for me. I'll bring the car and we can all go together."

As Jessica waited, outside in the garden for Mike, she called Sarah over her mobile phone. She told her what had happened and that they were headed to the doctor. Then she told her about the ylelow butterfly, the one they'd seen at the graveyard when they said goodbye to their mother Fran. It was back again, fluttering around Jessica.

It lay on Jessica's shoulder, as if trying to whisper in her ear.

Jessica told her sister about the butterfly as well.

Everything she had been through had finally made a believer out of Sarah. It was their mother's soul, she said, keeping a watch over you and the baby. She'd read up on the literature, even delving into ancient Egyptian alchemy.

Mike arrived in the car and Jessica said he would get in touch with her again once they were at the doctor's.

Jessica rushed into the car, and placed Adam safely in his special chair and tied the seatbelt around him then got into the front seat next to Mike only for him to race off.

Scene 4 – One Last Look

The gloomy, cloud-filled sky eventually burst into rains as Mike drove away. Then the winds become strong and lightning filled the air. Mike drove on not being able to concentrate on the road because he kept sneaking glances back at Adam to make sure he was okay. Then he took a sharp turns and the wheels screeched, with more raining pouring down on the metal of the car, like a wave, pushing down the branches of the surrounding trees to breaking point.

Mike turned to look at Adam again and found that the boy had closed his eyes from the fever that was ailing him. Jessica begged Mike to slow down but he couldn't. He was too afraid for their son. The windshield wipers weren't coping with the sheer amount of rain and it was hard to see the road. Mike pushed down on the peddle oblivious.

That's when a tree broke and fell in the middle of the road. He didn't see it and moved on straight towards it while another car raced ahead of him itself. The driver, seeing the tree, slammed the breaks and the car turned around Mike's vehicle before it flew up into the air like a leaf in the wind. Crashing into a concrete pylon, it came crashing down again, right into the front of Mike's car.

He tried to swerve out of the way and couldn't. He tried to slam the breaks but it was too late. The car was coming for him. He knew there was nothing he could do. The last moment of his life, he turned his body and tried to block the other vehicle tearing through his car, placing his arm over Jessica and staring back at Adam's sweet beautiful face for the very last time.

Chapter 16

Scene 1 – Last Will and Testament

Mike's side of the car was obliterated but despite that, he clung on as the sirens of the ambulances made their way to the harrowing accident, taking all the victims to the Brooklyn trauma centre. He was between life and death, breathing in his last, when they arrived.

It wasn't just the ambulances that were there. The press was in force too, creeping out of the woodwork given the cheer number of casualties. The names of the victims were blared on TV for all to see. That's when Sarah saw the news broadcast, collapsing from the sheer shock of hearing her sister's name, let alone Mike's. She ran to the car in her household clothes, racing to the trauma centre, eyes bleary with tears and hysteria.

She finally found the doctor in charge and pelted him with questions. Mike was gone. Jessica was in critical condition, with internal bleeding, while Adam was unharmed. But he was running a dangerous fever. Sarah rushed to Jessica's room only to find her lucid, eyes fixed on her infant son. Looking deeper into her eyes she could see the weaknesses drawing her away from her, her companion of all these years, the only one she had in the world after their mother had died.

Jessica blinked then closed her eyes, but she was aware of Sarah's presence in the room. She could hear her little sister's sobs. She opened her eyes all of a sudden and stretched out her arms for a final embrace. Sarah hugged her as Jessica spoke.

"Don't worry about me, little sis. I'm fine. I'll be seeing our mother soon. I'll ask her everything, about the secret of the yellow butterfly."

Then she fell silent for a moment, closing her eyes once again as if resting from the ordeal while Sarah continued to sob, shocking her own voice.

Jessica knew it was the end. There was nothing more for her in this world. Only what lay beyond.

Kevin and Ray and Sandy had made it their as well, barging their way into Jessica's room. They stood in silence. That's when Jessica mustered what little strength she had and pried her eyes open, directing her gaze at the nurse. "A pen and paper please," she said simply.

The nurse, a little dazed, did as she was told.

Jessica wanted to 'give up' Adam, to her sister Sarah. She wanted it down in black and white, her own last will and testament. She then told the nurse to hand over the paper to Sarah.

"Don't talk that way, you'll get better. You'll see," Sarah said in desperation.

"Don't you see," Jessica said weakly. "I fulfilled your dream. I got you Adam, your son. I just want you to promise."

"Anything," Sarah replied in tears.

"Promise you'll love him and cherish him and raise him. He has no one in the world except you. He's your son now."

The last flicker of life in her eyes finally departed that moment.

Sarah continued to stare transfixed at her sister as she departed this world, while the nurse tended to Adam, giving him an injection to reduce his temperature.

Sandy and Ray burst into tears, and even Kevin was moved. Jessica, beautiful Jessica, looked like she was asleep, like nothing had happened. Sarah took Adam from the nurse and hugged him as he too cried, aware in his own way that his mother was gone.

Some time later Kevin, Ray and Sandy left the room. Sarah came out, Adam in her arms. She spoke directly to Kevin, confronting him. "He's coming with me," she said. "Make your decision. Either Adam grows up with us, or it's over between us."

Kevin couldn't muster a reply and moved away from her instead. That's when she snapped and took the boy with her, heading back to Flabusht, to go back to being a doctor and dedicate her life to Adam the way Jessica had dedicated her life to her.

Scene 2 – Back to Flatbush

Sarah returned to her memories, old and new, now that she was back in Flatbush, in the home she'd grown up in, sleeping in the same bed she'd shared with Jessica after their mother had died. It was like everything in her life had been smashed, except for one thing. Adam.

She'd place him after night on Jessica's bed and tend to him, while she cried silently for what they'd both lost. Adam's health got better. He responded well to the medicine he was given and his temperature abated with time. The house felt so empty now that Jessica was gone. Every room, ever corner, held a memory of either her or their mother. Like the piano, or the fireplace, or the silver chandelier over the fireplace which they hadn't lit since their mother died, or the bookshelves that made up the small library.

The doorbell rang, startling her out of her memories. It was uncle Robert. She threw herself in his arms only to find he was just as distraught. First Fan, then Jessica. Sarah was all he had left of Fran and he was the closest thing she had to a father.

Not long after Ray and Sandy made their way to Flatbush to pay their respects and check up on her. Then Kevin came, by himself, but no sooner had he got there that someone else entirely came as well.

John Jr. Sarah threw herself into is arms as well. She didn't know why exactly she did that, but his own embrace was warm and tender and comforted her to no end. Kevin looked on, fuming.

Scene 3 – Back to the Meir Residence
Days went by as Sarah learned to cope with the shock of what had happened and Kevin eventually made his mind up to apologise for his lack of reaction and to accept Adam into his home. And so she retuned like a ship docking at a familiar port, the cargo of sorrows she carried with her forgotten, for the moment. Then Catherine interjected, seeing that Adam was here, a reminder of precisely what she disdained and what she'd brought her son up to disdain.

She didn't hurt the boy, wasn't directly cruel, but she neglected him, his cries, his desire to play with others. She wouldn't even let Rita handle him or care for him. On one occasion she actually stepped on his toys and broke them. Not that he had anything against her. He'd smile at her with his innocent face.

All Kevin could think to do was console his mother than this was a temporary arrangement. Sooner or later Adam would leave.

Catherine persisted, her mouth being her main weapon. Talking endlessly with her son about how this was all his fault, brining this little black brat here to be raised in the Meir mansion.

Scene 4 – Deprivation

When was the last time Kevin and Sarah had sex? He could scarcely remember. Since she'd been back, nothing had happened and for an inordinately long time. It was two things. First, Adam, then her work. On one particular occasion he'd planned for a romantic evening with her, as their anniversary was arriving. They both got dressed up for the occasion, eager to resume their love life, followed by hugs and kisses, followed by caresses, followed by Sarah taking her clothes in preparation for… then the sound of the Baby Monitor intruded. Adam was crying.

Sarah left Kevin and rushed to Adam's room, barely covering her nude body in the meantime. She stayed with him till he finally stopped crying and then dozed off on the bed beside him.

The morning after, Kevin woke up as grumpy as he had ever been in his life. He finally burst out at her, at the breakfast table: "Everything is Adam this, Adam that! What about me? Adam isn't even your son."

"Yes he is," she replied steadily. "I'll take care of him as long as there is breath in me."

She understood Kevin perfectly. It wasn't that Adam was taking up all her time. It was the colour of his skin.

As Kevin stewed in his own juices from that point on till he found himself, amazingly, missing Janet!

He found himself forgiving her. He found himself making excuses for her, believing that she was a victim in all this and it was her sorry excuse for a husband that was responsible for what she'd done to him. Sure she was a bitch, living the life of a prostitute for more than money – for the sex itself – but she gave a man what he wanted in exchange, whenever he wanted it. Could you blame her for answering the call of her flesh?

The only thing that stopped him going back to her was that he didn't have the time!

Two long years passed by and the situation didn't improve between them, with Catherine only making things worse. Sarah could see how Rita wasn't being allowed anywhere near Adam and how the boy was left alone in his bedroom whenever she was at the hospital.

Then she found Kevin holding the boy up high, apparently playing with him, but it looked like he was going to drop him on the floor and *kill* him.

'Are you mad," she screamed to a dumbfounded Kevin. "He's just a child. You could hurt him. Is that what you want? Is that how much you hate him just because he's Mike's son?" she stle the bow from his hands, checked that he was okay, then added: "Adam is staying with me, one way or another. Either accept it, and try and be a human being for once in your life, or give me a divorce."

Then she burst out of their room, out of the mansion entirely, and back to Flat Bush.

It was almost a relief. Things began returning to normal and it was good to be home, till the real shock came

She found herself, on a number of occasions, feeling dizzy and sick. She knew the telltale signs. She didn't even need to be a doctor for that.

She was pregnant!

Chapter 17

Scene 1 – Pregnancy and a Resumption

Sarah remained in Flatbush despite her pregnancy, some of the happiest days of her life with Adam to keep her company. She would play with him and coddle him and show him all the pictures of his parents, Jessica and Mike. She would tell him these are your parents and the boy, uncomprehending but innocent, would smile nonetheless, then caress her face with the soft skin of his hands.

The doorbell rang. Sarah made her way to the front door and found it was Sandy, with Ray standing behind her.

They always dropped by to check on her, especially after learning that she was adamant on breaking up with Kevin. They spent the whole time trying to convince her to return to Kevin, especially since she was in her sixth month of pregnancy. It was best that her new child be raised with both his parents, they said. When that didn't work they tried other tracks.

"Kevin loves you, Sarah," Sandy said.

"I know that" she replied. "But I can't stand him anymore. Adam is an orphan, and he's my responsibility. Who else does he have in the world? Who is going to take care of him? He's *my* son."

"Nobody said you should give him up," Ray consoled "He's coming with you, naturally."

"It won't work," Sarah retorted. "He can't sand him. And neither does Catherine."

Then a gentle knock came on the door and it turned out to be Kevin!

He came over, grovelling, wanting Sarah back at the Meir mansion, and with her Adam.

Even Ray, who'd spent the last few days avoiding Kevin thanks to his inexcusable behaviour – towards John Jr. and Adam – sided with Kevin to the point of actually standing right next to him.

Sarah didn't know what to think. She wanted Adam by her side but after the way Kevin had behaved, almost killing the child, she couldn't risk it.

"Give me until tomorrow," Sarah finally said.

She spent the whole night thinking about Adam. It was during this mental haze that she heard a voice, a familiar voice, saying the word 'Robert' over and over again. She got up in a start, looking around her, shivering in the cold, quiet night.

It was Fran. She was certain. "Uncle Robert," she said out load. "How could I have forgotten!"

She made her mind up to go to him. He was the ideal person to raise Adam. He was lonely and needed to love someone to give meaning to his life again. She'd go to him early next morning and also get Adam's nanny----FIX BEFORE-----. From that point onwards she could sleep in peace.

She called him early in the morning.

"Hallo," he said not knowing who it was at this hour of the day.

"It's me," Sarah replied.

"Sarah! I can't believe it," he said with transparent glee in his voice.

"I'm fine. How are you?"

"I'm alright. But it would be nice if you visited me once in a while, like your dear sister Jessica."

"I'll be there today," Sarah replied.

"You aren't pulling my leg," he said.

"Believe me, uncle Robert. I need you more than ever," she explained. "Adam is going to be staying with you. And his nanny."

The words fell on him unexpectedly, but he was so thrilled he couldn't reply straight away. Then he told her to stay put. He was the one who was coming over.

He dressed in a rush and made his way to the car with a youthful gait and drove off to Flat Bush. He couldn't believe this was happening, but it was, and he was thankful!

Later that day Sarah finally packed her bags and went back to the Meir residence, without Adam. Even with the new arrival growing inside her she missed Adam and couldn't stop thinking about him. She still lamented the fact that the boy would grow up far away from what was left of his family. That's why she made it a policy to head off to Robert's, every single day, to see Adam and play with him and check on uncle Robert.

Robert was finally in good shape. He had something to do with his life, and he was taking care of the boy who was Jessica's son, all that was left of her, the dear girl who'd looked after him for all this time since Fran died. He stopped drinking and smoking and actually began to take care of himself, his appearance, and where he lived. The house was full of love and light and colours once more. His health improved, his diet improved – with some help from the nanny, to be honest – and his mental health improved. He finally had a family of his own, people to care for, and people to take care of him. He was finally becoming human again!

He devoted himself to Adam, to the boy's education, teaching him the alphabet for starters, and playing with him and getting him toys. No more lonely nights for him. Even when he recollected Fran, and now Jessica, it was no longer with a sense of loss, for they were here with him now and he could express his love for them in the best way possible, by caring for Adam.

Sarah, for her part, had to endure being far away from Adam, when she was at the Meir residence, and endure the growing pains of pregnancy, and endure Catherine.

"Take care of yourself and don't waste any more time on Adam," she'd say to her. And Kevin would pitch in too, repeating his mother's wisdom.

"He may be black but he's a human being, just like you. Remember that," Sarah threw back defiantly.

And so the same problems that had existed before in the Meir mansion resumed themselves, with endless bickering and arguments between Sarah and Kevin, and Catherine, with frosty relations and emotional recrimination. The only time that Sarah was happy was when she went over to Robert's to spend hours and hours with Adam, while Robert regaled her with his memories of Fran.

On one occasion, while at Robert's, she felt pains, so Robert took her speedily in his car to the Meir residence. Only to receive a cavalcade of recriminations from Catherine. Kevin, rushing down the stairwell, joined in the insults, only for Sarah to faint from the sheer agony she was suffering. That shut Kevin up.

He rushed to the hospital in his car and the medical personnel proceeded to place her on the stretcher to take her into the emergency room.

The next few minutes were agony as Kevin waited and waited, sweating and stressed out of his mind, only to hear the cries of his baby in the distance as the nurse came out and congratulate him. He forced his way in and proceeded to kiss Sarah over and over again.

She'd given a normal birth with no complications this time. And the result was a perfectly healthy boy, whom she named Andy.

Scene 2 – Catherine's Transformation

Catherine, now in her fifties, was finally satisfied in her life. She had a grandchild, her son was happy and everything she'd lost thanks to her husband's betrayal and John Jr. and Liz had been compensated for by the hand of fate. She hadn't been able to sleep well over the previous period, constantly waking up when she'd be plagued by dreams of her husband having sex with attractive old Liz. He'd do it with Liz, right in front of her in the Meir residence, in her nightmare, and Liz would stare her in the face every single time, smiling and moaning at the same time. Catherine would burst into tears in her dreams and wake up to find herself crying in real life. The only thing that kept her gong was the quest for revenge.

She made her mind up to enjoy herself, with her husband's money, what was left of it, and began making her way to beauty clinics and plastic surgeons. She was her old self again in no time at all.

That's when she began to leave the mansion, every chance she got, and began frequenting clubs and meeting with women her own age who'd also found ways to cope with loneliness, talking about nothing but relationships and sex. It all stocked the flames of her forlorn femininity, for so long unsatisfied thanks to John Meir's illness.

That's when she chanced on some unemployed young man, seducing him with money, and spending a few nights away from the mansion. Kevin couldn't help but notice. He didn't press he on the issue but he became attuned to it.

Catherine had a rendezvous planned with her young man at a seedy motel. Little did she know that Kevin was in pursuit, following her since she left the mansion. He found where she was going. He saw her in the window of the room she'd rented. He couldn't take it anymore. He barged into the motel, rushed up the stairs and burst into the room to find his mother kissing a boy who was even younger than he was, while the youth was busily getting undressed.

Kevin grabbed him by the neck and dragged him to the floor, Catherine looking on in abject terror. The boy made a run for it, racing down the stairs with his trousers down, running for his life. She begged him not to hurt the boy, only for Kevin to unleash on his mother, using the rudest language imaginable.

In the end, he calmed down, and said, "If you want to get married because you're lonely, then get married. But don't do this and humiliate yourself and humiliate me!"

Then he turned and left.

Chapter 18

Scene 1 – Andy's Birthday

The Meir mansion was filled with the sounds of jubilation as the young celebrated Andy's nineteenth birthday. A spoilt boy standing amongst his friends, broad shouldered and tall and overly energetic, as those his age invariably were. He kept shifting from one spot to the next during the whole occasion, chatting with friends loudly, adding to the noise of champagne glasses clinking and the voices of boys and the seductive laughs of the attractive girls there. The tightly dressed or scantily clad girls there, one should add, girls there to show off their legs and breasts, in line with the festive mood of the occasion.

Everybody was white, girls and boys alike. And they were there to have unbridled fun. Instead of worrying themselves about finding secluded locations at university to enjoy themselves in – behind the shade of a tree, in a deserted classroom – whenever someone got a little bit too drunk over here, all they had to do was excuse themselves and go and rest in one of the many guest rooms in the Meir residence and enjoy themselves there. Andy was one of them, heading to just such a room with a girl – he didn't even know her name – and enjoyed themselves, with the help of a satchel of drugs. The only thing that blotted out the moans, and screams, was the noise of the party below. It left the place looking like the seedy hotel where Janet operated out of.

It was still 8pm. The party had started at five. Kevin was still at his company and Sarah still at the hospital, on purpose. So the young could have their day. The music, the laughter, the bright lights of the party made themselves felt in and out of the Meir residence. It was at that point that Sarah's car parked in the garage. She could clearly hear what was going on inside.

While she didn't voice any objections to what was happening, Andy made it a point to cool things down a bit. He greeted her as a son should, only for her to see the rings under his eyes. Still, she didn't scold him. She knew exactly what he was getting up to. She just went upstairs to be by herself and worry silently about her son and the carefree life of drugs and decadent abandon he was living, and what effect it was having on his studies.

What could she do? She'd tried over and over again, taking him to rehab, to no avail. It was at about this time that she began devoting herself more and more to Adam, as if unconsciously compensating for the failures of her son. Adam was going from strength to strength in his studies and had finally joined the Brooklyn academy, following on from his dear mother Jessica. He was a natural at music and song, joining the church choral. He didn't even need to sing with the choir, his voice was strong and pleasant enough for him to do all the singing by himself, to the jubilation of everyone at church – the worshippers and the people that worked there.

On one particular occasion Sarah had been there, with Robert, and also with Nancy, Adam's friend and choir mate. Sarah couldn't help but notice the girl afterwards. She simply had to ask.

"A friend and a colleague," Adam said innocently.

Nancy took the cue and greeted Sarah herself. She was a well to do girl, Sarah could see. Not pompous like an aristocrat but certainly groomed and elegant.

Robert was ecstatic himself. He'd raised the boy from his infancy and considered him to be more than a son. He was his best friend, keeping him company in his old age. He was pushing seventy. Nothing could make him happier than to see Adam with the right kind of girl. She had a moon-shaped face, white with rosy cheeks, and eyes so blue that the sea was jealous of her.

Robert and Sarah wisely decided to take themselves out of the picture and leave Adam and Nancy to themselves. The young couple painted the town red that night, only to sit down in a quiet place and have a philosophical discussion about love and relationships. Nancy was transfixed, speaking romantically about love with his sense of manly confidence and his gentleness, with his features finely chiselled in black stone and his green as grass eyes.

Her hand extended to take him. That was the first time they had truly touched, a testament that the boundary that had lay between them no longer existed. They were in love and wanted the world to know it. All is fair in love and war, as the saying goes.

That's when the kisses began.

Scene 2 – Adam Confesses

Robert was looking through the papers that day. Five police officers had been killed, in revenge for the shooting of a black kid the day before. He knew that things were precarious. He was worried about Adam but in an effort to hide his fears he asked him instead about Nancy.

Adam, the closest thing to a son he had in this world, confessed outright that he was in love with her.

Robert attempted more subterfuge, wise in his old age. "You never told me anything about her before. Who is she? Where does she come from?"

"In Manhattan," Adam replied innocently.

Shaking his head, cunningly, Robert said, "She seems to be a rich girl then. I know quite a few of the wealthy families there. Which one does she belong to?"

"Richard Falkner, the man running for the Senate. She's his daughter."

Robert's features tightened all of a sudden, but he forced his face back to normal as quickly as he could. He didn't want Adam to suspect anything. He followed this up with a fake smile, to himself time to think. They resumed the conversation but talked only about the girl and how pretty she was and how quiet and elegant. He could see just how happy Adam was.

He called Sarah the following day and asked her to drop by while Adam was at the academy. She got permission from the hospital to head out for a bit. As soon as she got to his house, she pressed the buzzer persistently, worried about what he might want her for.

"What is it uncle Robert," she said in a hurry when he opened the door.

"And hallo to you too," he replied before greeting her in.

"What is it," Sarah continued in the same tone.

"Nothing, nothing at all." He waited for her to sit down first. "Do you remember Nancy? Adam's choir mate."

"Yes," she replied.

"Do you have any idea whose daughter she is?"

"No," she said factually.

Then when the worry became evident in his voice. "Richard Falkner."

"The man running for the Senate," she asked.

"Yes, one and the same," he replied.

"And what does Adam have to do with all this?"

"He's in love with her and it seems she's in love with him too," Robert explained.

"Love!" she said loudly. "Couldn't he find anyone else to fall in love with. Does he have any idea who she is?"

"I'm afraid he does," he replied. "But it's love."

"What are we going to do about it," Sarah said.

"We can't rush into this," he explained. "Just, first off, don't tell him I said anything to you. When he gets back from the academy, just strike up a conversation with him and let him bring up Nancy."

Not long after that Adam came home. He was a little surprised to find Sarah there at this time of day but he was so overjoyed he didn't think anything of it. For her part Sarah embraced him and greeted him warmly, telling him how much she missed him and so she just had to drop by today.

Robert got the coffee brewing in the meantime, his ears on the roaming conversation.

"By the way," Sarah said. "Who was that nice girl we saw at the church? The one you spent so much time with, your colleague?"

"Nancy," Adam replied.

"Is she just your colleague?" she teased.

"No, we've been seeing each other for quite some time now. We're planning to go serious."
"So you love her," Sarah asked.
"And she loves me," he replied.
"Who is her father," Sarah said innocently.
Robert had brought the coffee by then. But he didn't serve it. He just sat down, preoccupied, waiting for the punchline.
Adam said who her father was and Sarah, feigning surprise, replied, "But… couldn't find someone else to get involved with."
"And what's wrong with her," he asked uncomprehending.
"Mr Falkner is political, and he's not very friendly towards black people, although he won't admit to it. You can be sure you won't be welcome in his house." She hated to say it but she had to. Adam was her son.
"But why?" Adam said.
"Because your father was black," she said as gently as she could.
"And my mother was white," he retorted.
"It's different. Nobody stood in the way of your dear mother Jessica, but this man definitely will."
That's when Robert finally interjected, following on from where Sarah left off.

"Adam, my son," he said gently, placing his hand on Adam's shoulder. "Choose anyone your want. Just don't get yourself into trouble." Yesterday's headlines were still fresh in his mind.

"It would be better to forget her," Sarah resumed the conversation. "Can you promise me that?"

Tears made their tentative way from Adam's eyes. He marshalled what strength he had and promised them both.

Then he got up and went to his room to be by himself.

Scene 3 – Nancy Falls in Love

Nancy was driving her car home across Wall Street, the black steering wheel bringing up the delicate whiteness of her fingers and the lovely smoothness of her hands. She was full of zest, for her love of Adam, recollecting how their hands grouped each other and how their fingers interlocked, exaggerating and accentuating their budding love for each other.

She was also thinking about her father, however. What he would do if he found out about them and how they didn't 'match' each other. The two contradictory impulses battled themselves out in her to the point of exhaustion. Even when she was home, she couldn't sleep from the delicious elixir of Adam's love and the dread she felt from her father.

Seeing herself in Adam's eyes, imagining his broad shoulders and barrel chest, was beyond bearing She'd tried, resisted, falling in love with her for so long, but he brought out the woman in her, finally putting an end to the girl that had always been there. She wasn't just in love with him. She was *addicted* to him.

Moving around restlessly on her bed she imagined herself talking to him. She extended her hand to her bedside table, opening the drawer to take out a photo she had of him.

How distinct he was. Dark skinned with green eyes and a face that wasn't entirely black. She had to see him again, whatever her father would think. Then she remembered that tomorrow was thanksgiving. No school tomorrow!

She looked outside her bedroom window, through the stained glass which turned her room into a rainbow of possibilities.

Chapter 19

Scene 1 – Tit for Tat

The early morning hours passed all too quickly in preparation for Thanksgiving, the most routine of which was getting the potatoes ready and the turkey, which was centre stage in the banquet. At the dinner table was Richard and his daughter, his one and only child, Nancy, and with her her mother Monica. In was right in the middle of the festivities, when her father had a sizeable piece of Turkey in his mouth, that Nancy surprised him with the question: "Dad, what would you think if I had a relationship with a black man?"

He didn't seem to comprehend that his daughter was being serious. "Nancy, my dear. Would you pass the potatoes. This is more important!"

He continued to munch away continently, not entirely aware of what his daughter had just said.

Nancy understood, however, that the whole topic was taboo. She busied herself with slicing a piece of meat on her plate, pretending to be hungry and swallowing her emotions instead of the food.

Not that anything would stop her meeting with Adam. Her father's silence almost encouraged her, as if he wasn't approving her plans but not disapproving them.

They met, and met, and met, at the academy and elsewhere, and every time she was drawn closer and closer to him. They met with friends, they met by themselves, they met on the coast of the Atlantic ocean, enjoying the view and the breeze and each other's company. In the city lights at night her face turned from white to silver, drawing words out of Adam that inflamed their passion all the more. He couldn't resist her any more than she could resist him.

Meanwhile, Richard Falkner began to wonder about what his daughter had said on Thanksgiving. His wife told him that to her knowledge Nancy had got involved with a black boy, and from the Meir family… He cut her off at that point. "There aren't any Negros in the Meir family," he said sternly.

From that point onwards, he had his guards follow Nancy wherever she went, but to be discreet so she didn't suspect anything. And so they tracked her every move, from home to the academy to Manhattan to Central Park, photographing her and Adam in secret as they met, talked, held hands, hugged and kissed.

Richard almost blew his top off when he saw the pictures. Revenge was the only thing on his mind, now he directed his guards to gather everything they could on this boy.

All the guards had to do was head off to the academy to get all the information they needed. When he was born, where he lived, how long he'd been at the academy. It wasn't long before Richard made his way, with his guards, to Robert's house.

Robert opened the door not expecting what lay outside. It was like seeing an angry cop at your front porch. He'd never in his life thought that something like this could happen to him, with such a bigwig on his doorstep. He was quite literally shaking in his boots.

The ungrateful guest refused to sit down the whole time he was there. He didn't even bother to introduce himself.

All Robert could think to do was call on Adam to come here right this minute from your room and leave whatever it is you're doing!

"Tell your *boy* to stay away from my daughter, get it," Richard said as soon as Adam made his presence felt. "Do you have any idea who I am? Do you have any idea who *you* are," he added.

Adam tried to respond, angrily, but Robert 'convinced' him to stay quite. He filled in for Adam instead. "There... seems to be some misunderstanding in all this..." his teeth chattered as he spoke.

"And who do you think *you* are, you old coot," Richard yelled.

As luck would have it, Sarah was making her way to Robert's as part of her weekly routine, checking on the both of them. She could just about hear what was going on inside. As scared as she herself was, she couldn't stop herself barging in to confront Richard and his guards.

She recognised the man straight away. Even if she hadn't seen his picture in the news, she could guess who he was. The guards standing either side of him looked like a pair of muscular genies.

She had some yelling of herself to do. "How dare you threaten my son! Who gave you permission to set foot here? Get out right this minute before I call the cops, you phony!"

The man preached the gospel of equality and justice, while running for public office. In private, he was a whole different animal.

"And who do you think you are," was all Richard could think to say.

"I'm a doctor, I'll have you know. Sarah Meir." He was somewhat taken aback. He didn't imagine a woman could be so *composed*. Instead of get into a war of words, he left as suddenly as he came.

"Didn't I warn you," Robert said as quietly as he could. He was still shaking from the inside. "You promised us."

Sarah joined in, despite her bravado moments ago. "Aren't you at least afraid for yourself?"

"I'm sorry, mum. But we're in love," said Adam.

"The problem isn't with *her*, it's with her father. Can't you see? He came here and threatened you, in your home," she tried to explain.

He swallowed his pride and broke it off with Nancy.

Days passed by at the academy with Adam doing his best to avoid even bumping into here. But Nancy wouldn't give up. She was in hot pursuit and eventually confronted him.

"Why are you avoiding me? Don't you love me anymore, or it someone else?" she said.

He couldn't help himself. He hugged her. He missed her so much.

She could clearly see that something was wrong. "What is it?" she asked melodiously.

"It was your father. He threatened me. He called me a Negro!"

She couldn't believe her ears. There were tears in Adam's eyes. He was saying the truth. All her father's electioneering, all the lies. She'd just seen the true, ugly face of her father.

Drawing the golden fleece of her hair backwards in a bold move, she said, "Well, I'm not giving up, Adam. And neither are you. We love each other and my father won't come between us no matter what!"

Little did she know that her father's men were watching her right this minute, relaying everything back to their boss in real-time, and in detail.

Scene 2 – A Surprise that Turned All the Tables

Richard, even in his rage, remembered what Monica had told him. Adam was from the Meir family. And so he went to the Meir company to meet with the patriarch of the family, Kevin.

For his part Kevin had no idea Richard Falkner, *the* Richard Falkner, was coming to see him today. He just assumed the man was on the campaign trail and looking for financiers, so he gave him a warm welcome and invited him into his office.

That's when he surprised him about Adam and Nancy. He said he was worried about the relationship getting into the press, something he couldn't allow to happen this close to polling day. He would do anything to terminate the relationship.

After recovering momentarily from the shock of what was happening Kevin gave his guest a sly grin. "I'm with you," he said. "You won't *believe* what I've suffered because of his father."

"How exactly are you two connected," Richard asked.

"He's my wife's nephew."

"Then that's go after him together," Richard said expectantly.
"It's a deal," Kevin said.
Richard went out to his car and returned to his home in Wall Street. He had his own plans about Nancy. She was to be grounded, indefinitely. Practically put under house arrest.
Days passed and Nancy remained on her bed, face in her hands, crying. Her mother, by her side, tried to console her. "You'll forget him," Monica said. "Just give it time."
Nancy continued to cry.
"Love is always hard," Monica continued. "You'll get over it. This is your first time. That's all."
Monica got up to leave. When she was out of earshot, Nancy called Adam. Sobbing she confessed to him. She was pregnant!
Adam's eyes almost popped out of his head when he heard those words.
"Don't leave me Adam I love you. I can't live without you," she continued.
Adam placed the receiver down. His head was spinning.

He focused and focused, trying to figure out what to do. Her voice snapped him out it. "Adam, Adam. Did you hear me?"

He couldn't breathe let alone think. Thank heavens Sarah entered his room at just that minute.

He didn't hear her enter, which she noted, so she asked him what was the matter. He spilled the beans,

It took her a little time to digest the news herself but, with her trademark wisdom and gentleness, He placed her hand on his shoulder to reassure him. "We'll find a way out, I promise you," she finally said.

Later that day she was back at the Meir residence, raking her brains. She figured out what needed to be done. She would contact Monica.

On a bright and sunny day that Spring, when was sure what she needed to do and say, Sarah contacted Monica. She greeted her and asked if this was a good time to talk. Monica replied in the affirmative, asking who this was.

"Sarah Meir," Sarah replied, before adding, "Adam's aunt."

"I see," said Monica. "We'll I'm pleased to make your acquaintance. We really should meet. We've got so much to talk about. Nancy has certainly told me a great deal about you."

"You are exactly right. We really should meet," said Sarah. "Could we, say, meet in the evening to have dinner together. We could chat about Adam and Nancy. I know the perfect place."

It was a done deal.

They met at 7pm at the Falten and McDougal intersection.

Sarah was at the hospital thinking over what they would talk about, so the hours passed by all too quickly. She excused herself a little early and drove to Falten and McDougal----, when she arrived she called Monica on her mobile, since neither of them knew what the other looked like.

"I'm the one standing in front of the red car, wearing jeans," Sarah explained.

Monica was in her forties and not as slender as she used to be, but a sophisticated and good looking woman nonetheless, with sharp brown eyes.

"You must be Sarah," she said when she saw Sarah in her faded jeans. "And you must be Monica!"

Chapter 20

Scene 1 – Finding a Solution

Restaurants were evenly spread around the intersection, exuding pleasant smells of frying and grilling to open up people's appetites to no end. Their feet drew them to the quieter species of restaurant and sat at a table. That's how they broke any ice that may have set them apart, which was customary when it came to a first meeting. Not long after they felt like they'd know each other for years and years. The conversation proceeded just as smoothly, moving from one topic to the next, till Sarah finally got to the point.

"Dear Monica, I feel like we're friends already. We can't keep avoiding the problem, thinking it will drift away by itself. You may not know a great deal about me, but you will with time. This won't be the last time we meet, I wager. What concerns me before anything is Adam. He grew up an orphan. His father and his mother, my sister Jessica, died in a car accident. He's just like my son, Andy. And you know how much your daughter loves Adam. It's not just puppy love." Sarah paused for a moment, measuring what she would say. "She's pregnant."

Before Monica had a chance to react the waiter came to their table and offered them today's menu. Sarah took it upon herself to order for both of them, seeing the effect her words had had on Monica. (Just some juice and pastries). The words had been like thunder in her ears. Her head was full of questions. What would her husband do if he found out?

Her head looked like it was going to fall off so Sarah added, "Please, Monica, what's happened has happened. There's nothing we can do to undo it. We have to confront the situation, wisely, so nobody gets hurt."

"How could this happen," Monica finally said. "I can't think! You have no idea what Richard is like, how he hates black people. If he knew his daughter was carrying Adam's child."

"I'm *well* aware of what Richard is like. He was at Adam's house and threatened him to his face," Sarah explained. "He only left when I threatened to call the police. Richard needs to know. That's the only way."

"Then leave it to me," Monica said. "I'll be in touch."

They rose from their table before the waiter came back with their order and went their separate ways. Monica's head felt like it would burst on the drive back. The first thing she did after she parked her car was head up to her daughter's room, finding her lying on her bed, distraught and sickly. She loved Adam that much that it was affecting her physical health, and the threatening the health of the baby that was growing up inside her. Adam's baby. She had to break her silence and confront Richard. She couldn't risk losing her daughter.

It couldn't have come at a worse time. Richard was exhausted. The electioneering was getting to him and it was late anyway. She gathered together her courage and said, as calmly as possible, "Richard, we have to talk."

"Please Monica," his reply was drowsy and bored. "Can't it wait till the morning."

"No, it can't," she surprised herself by saying. "We're losing our daughter, Richard. Why can't you just let her marry the man she loves? Why are you standing in the way of her happiness? She loves Adam and won't give him up. You've been doing nothing but pursue your dreams, this damn election, for so long you've forgotten about us." She paused for a moment before she broke into tears. "I'm scared, Richard. Nancy may kill herself."

"No," came the simple reply. He wasn't compromising with anybody, even those closest to him.

"You don't have a choice," Monica said firmly.

"What do you mean," Richard wondered. She'd never spoken to him this way before.

"You don't have a choice," she repeated. "We don't have a choice. Nancy's pregnant. From Adam"

"What are you saying?"

"You heard me," Monica retorted.

Richard's legs suddenly felt weak. He slouched over into a chair before he could fall. "That's impossible," he finally said.

"It's the truth. We've got no choice. We have to deal with it," Monica continued.

His face suddenly turned murderous. "Then she has to get an abortion."

"Do you think she'd agree to that," Monica replied. "She's 22 years old. We can't force her into anything."

"And what if the baby came out…," his voice trailed off. He couldn't abide the word 'black'.

"Then that's our fate," Monica said.

Scene 2 – Two Friends Conspire

The windows that day were jittering from the chill of the early morning air. Monica hadn't been able to sleep at all. The first thing she did when she got up was call Sarah to tell her what happened last night.

Sarah was furious when she heard what Richard Falkner wanted to do. "You tell him…," she tried to steady her voice before continuing, "if he tries that then I'll call the police. I'm going to defend that baby, Adam's baby, to the very end."

"I'm with you my dear," Monica replied. "I'd never let him hurt my only daughter. All I want is for Nancy to be happy."

"Then we're agreed," Sarah said.

Monica returned to her daughter in the girl's bedroom. Nancy saw that her mother was smiling.

"No more tears," Monica said. "I've met Sarah, Adam's aunt. We just spoke on the phone today. We'll do anything we can to make sure you marry Adam."

Nancy's eyes lit up from that point onwards. She swerved herself around in a start and hugged her mother for all she was worth. There were still tears in her eyes but from happiness now. The old Nancy was back.

As for Sarah, things were going badly for her and Kevin. They were drifting apart, physically. He'd yelled at her, more than once, "All you care about is that Negro!"

"That Negro has a name. And I've told you over and over again that I'm never abandoning him."

"What don't you pay more attention to your son. He's become an addict," he replied.

"You destroyed Andy. You spoilt him rotten and I warned you about that. You never had any time for him. All you can think about is your company and John Jr. now our son is in Rehab. What good did your money do him in the end?" she said angrily.

"You're the one that destroyed our life, and everybody around us," Kevin threw back at her.

"That's enough." Sarah replied. She got up in a start, ears in her eyes, and went to her own room in the Meir residence. She'd been sleeping in a separate room for some time now. Whenever they met, in bed, they argued, so naturally they drifted apart.

Kevin, afterwards, was in the study, all by himself, frustrated and angry. That's when he recollected Janet and his incredible night with her. A prostitute no doubt but she was someone who helped you forget everything, all your troubles and everything else. She poured her body into you like wine in a glass. He'd have to look her up some time.

Scene 3 – Kevin Returns to Janet

Over the years Kevin had learned how to handle this breed of people, whether prostitutes or their pimps. But Janet always stood out in his mind. After a prolonged session of thinking about it he finally decided to make his way to where they'd last met, all those years ago, when her husband had shown up to squeeze money out of him. She was *that* good in bed it was worth the indignity, Kevin reasoned, and so he was back at the hotel, at the bar, waiting to see if she still worked there. Sipping on a glass of whiskey, he quietened what was left of his conscious, and drowned out his remaining sense of dignity. His eyes roamed the establishment, looking for a familiar face, only for the scent of a woman to intrude on his senses. A familiar scent.

It was Janet, smoking a cigarette, her favourite brand, with an elegant and elongated filter, her lipstick evident on it. "Don't I know you from somewhere?" she asked casually.

"It's Kevin," he replied.

"Ahh, yes. The billionaire's son. How could I forget?" Leaning towards him, she added, "Do you want another night like our last night together? Is that what you're here for?"

She proceeded to describe the organs she would stimulate in their upcoming enterprise. The words, and images, registered on Kevin's eyes.

In an effort to calm himself down he said, "Haven't you forgotten about someone? The man who threatened me after our night together, and then tried to blackmail me the day we buried my father. Steve, your husband."

"Please don't remind me," Janet replied. He's a criminal and I have to do what he says. I've got nowhere to live except this place." She gestured to the bar. "So please forgive me. But, what are you doing here anyway?"

"Don't you know?" he said.

"Sweet memories," she asked.

"Yes, that's it," Kevin confessed as best as he could. "So, where is your husband?"

He gave the barman an extra tip so that no one would disturb them as they spoke.

"He's out of town, robbing someone I suppose. The point it, he won't be take for a while," she said like the nymphomaniac that she was.

They had quite a night together. They assumed every position imaginable and she rode him like a thoroughbred, to the point of exhaustion. He barely made it back to his mansion in one piece, tripping over himself from the sheer effort and the amount of drink he'd consumed.

He found Sarah sitting in front of the TV set watching a press conference for Richard Falkner, giving a speech about freedom and equality and justice. He had guards with him, as always, but they were black this time.

"Ladies and gentlemen," he went on, "the age of slavery is over once and for all, I assure you. It's about time that the black man enjoys full equality across the entire country. It's time we erase this heritage of discrimination. We must champion the cause of the common man, not here alone but around the world."

The press conference was in front of Richard's house. Nancy was on the inside watching events as they unfolded on TV, following every word her father threw down to the audience. She couldn't take it anymore. "Lies, lies!" she screamed at the top of her voice, making a run for it outside the house, in front of the all the reports and correspondents.

"Lies, lies," she went on. "Everything my father says is a lie. He doesn't believe a word of what he's saying!"

The audience ignored her father and went after her, the cameras zooming in on her sweet, circular face. "My father is a phoney," she said. "He hates… Negros, as he calls them. He won't let me marry the man I love, a black man, just because of the colour of his skin. And I'm pregnant from him. He wanted me to give up the baby, abort my baby, because he's afraid the baby will be born black!"

Then she broke down and cried.

Richard almost fainted. He couldn't believe what just happened. She's just terminated his whole political career. Every news channel in the state, if not the country, would repeat what she'd said over and over again. It was all over. It was the scandal of the century.

Chapter 21

Scene 1 – Defeat and Hope
Richard felt defeated more as a person than a politician. He'd been assaulted by the closest person to him. The shock and pain was unbearable. Where did I go wrong, he asked himself over and over again, like a mad man? But the more he blamed Nancy, the more he found that he was to blame. He was the liar. He was the phoney. Most of all, he was the racist.

That's when Monica walked in on him, in his solitude, hearing voices in the winds. "Did I tell you we were losing our daughter," she said. "Why couldn't you just let her marry the man she loves? It would have spared us all this trouble."

He was sweating all over, his muscles suddenly turning weak in every nook and cranny of his body. The only part of him that kept functioning was his political instinct. He knew it was all over. He'd lost the election before they even announced the result.

They made the announcement the following day. He'd lost, a crushing defeat, despite the considerable lead he'd originally had. What had turned the tide against him? The black residents of Brooklyn who had originally been voting for him, with all his high and mighty claims of championing the common man and calling for equality.

Monica tried her best to console him, embracing him like he was her child who'd just woken up from a bad dream.

During these tumultuous events, Adam was prepping himself for his own big night – the talent contest he'd been waiting for, training for, all these years at the academy. He was more composed than he thought possible, sure of himself and his musical abilities. Sarah certainly had confidence in him, encouraging him all these years. That's why she didn't hesitate for a second to hand in a CD with his songs for the contents, on his behalf, without him even knowing about it.

Sarah, in point of fact, was at Robert's place, watching a repeated broadcast of the election result. It didn't take her and Robert, too long to put two and two together and figure out what happened to Richard.

Adam had been in the kitchen, getting coffee ready, but he heard what was going on the TV in the living room. He brought three steaming cups of coffee and the three of them reminisced on what had just happened. Sarah had only one thing to say. It was divine retribution, pure and simple.

When he entered and saw what was on TV, Adam, good natured person that he was, actually found himself feeling sorry for the man. He'd put his one meeting with Richard out of his mind and focused on the challenge ahead.

"You've got more to think about than the contest," Sarah chided. "There's also your baby with Nancy. And you have no reason to pity this man. He wanted to kill your baby, hurt his own daughter."

Everybody was hurting everybody else, in this life, Adam thought to himself. Sarah had told him about how Kevin and Catherine had treated him as a baby. He was too young to remember. When did it ever end, he pondered. How lucky he had been, in this life, to have Sarah and Robert. They were the parents he'd never had. Loving and rewarding him and sacrificing their personal happiness for him. He was more blessed than anyone in this life, and for that he was thankful.

Then Sarah made her big announcement, which was that she'd given the contest his CD. Adam was overjoyed, hugging her violently. Meanwhile Robert placed his hand on Adam's shoulder. "Don't worry about a thing," he said. "I'm sure you'll get everything you deserve."

Yes, Adam was truly blessed, with two angels by the names of Sarah and Robert.

Sarah, sadly, had to leave. She had her own responsibilities with her own family, although she much preferred it here. It was raining that night and she drove carefully back to the dingy place that the Meir mansion had finally become. Treading carefully once she was in, she overheard her husband talking to his mother. They were in Kevin's office.

Kevin's voice rose as he said the name John Jr. The man, technically his brother, had got out of hand. He'd bought shares costing close to half of the company's budget.

"This moron. This *maniac*," he went on, "wants to pilfer away my inheritance." Even Ray wasn't happy with John Jr.'s rash decision.

"You made him. You let him become the tyrant that he is," Catherine threw back at him.

"Not for much longer," Kevin said, biting his tongue.

Sarah, still in earshot, didn't comprehend that last sentence, but it filled her with dread.

Scene 2 – Kevin's Plots Against his Brother

Early the next day Kevin went straight to John Jr.'s office. "How dare you squander the company money on your hairbrained schemes," he said in one go, declining to say hallo or good morning as he barged into the office.

"You're a doctor," John Jr. replied calmly. "What would you know about business?"

Ray entered the office at the point, having overheard the altercation. For once, Ray sided with Kevin, if politely. John Jr. stared at the both of them bewildered. Neither seemed to understand what sense it made to buy shares at a cheap price, only to sell them afterwards when their price had risen.

"I took the right choice. Sooner, or later, you'll see the wisdom of my actions, for the company and for *us*," he added.

That's when the chest pains began. He had to excuse himself.

He left the building, racing in his car as he struggled to breathe, as if pulling in air through a pinhole. When he finally got to his apartment, he took his pills and calmed down. Later he spoke to his mother, Liz, and told her what had happened.

They day passed and Kevin had only one thing on his mind. John Jr. The reel of his memories wouldn't depart him. He remembered when he'd first met him at Edward's office. He'd remembered the scandalous press conference outside the company building. He remembered how the fans, and the shareholders, had fallen in love with the young upstart, congratulating for stealing Kevin's money. He remembered how his employees had been won over, one by one, to John Jr.'s side, the charming little chameleon that he was. That's how the seeds had been sown, and now they were in full bloom.

He had to do something and now.

He made a phonecall, to Janet.

She was ecstatic, thinking this was another one of their romantic rendezvous. They agreed on a time and the usual place.

Not long after he was at the bar. He'd driven faster than he should in the rainy weather, but he was a man possessed. She greeted like the sexual kitten that she was and embraced her hungrily.

"Our room is ready," she said luridly while grabbing his arm and trying to drag him up the stairs. She wanted him to put out the fire burning between her thighs.

"Not tonight," he replied, shocking her. "I'm here for something else. Something important."

"What could be more important than this," she said.

"Where's Steve," he replied, startling her.

"And what do you want him for," she inquired, puzzled.

Now Kevin grabbed her from her arm and took her to a secluded table, where they could speak in privacy. He wanted to *hire* Steve for something.

Somebody was threatening his life, he explained, so he needed some outside help.

Whore or not, she loved Kevin and wouldn't let anyone touch a hair on his head, so she arranged for a meeting between the two, her lover and her husband.

The night of the meeting, Kevin met Steve at his own hideout, a bar full of pimps like himself. He almost didn't believe that Kevin would show up, in a place like this to meet someone like him – given their history together.

"Hallo, Steve," Kevin said condescendingly, as Janet sat by his side.

"Mr Kevin wants to hire you for a job," she explained trying to dissuade her husband's doubts.

"I'm all ears," he finally said.

"I want you to get rid of somebody for me," Kevin stated bluntly.

"Murder ain't my scene," Steve replied abruptly. "I'm a conman, and a couple of other things. but I ain't a hired gun."

"You have connections," Kevin persisted.

"It's going to cost you," Steve said encouragingly.

"I'll give you all you want, and more," Kevin said with certainty.

Steve, weighing his words carefully, said, "In that case. Give me everything you have on this man you want gone. Name, where he works, lives. His daily routine. I need everything."

Kevin nodded eagerly. He only wanted to know when he would be killed.

"In a week or so," Steve replied.

"And how much are you willing to pay," Steve asked.

"Fifty thousand."

Steve's eyes glittered from the number. He'd hit the jackpot.

Scene 3 – Accepted into the Contest

The great American talent show sent him a letter confirming that he'd been accepted and telling him when he was expected there along with the other contestants. He only had a few days to stand up against both the audience and the judges. He sent an SMS to Nancy so she could watch him on TV. She was still being kept at home by her father, suffering in silence as she missed being with Adam so much. The baby growing inside her reminded Nancy of Adam all the more, especially know that the child was beginning to kick.

Some days later Richard was in his own self-styled prison, torturing himself with questions after his resounding failure at the polls. What did I do this to myself? What did I punish my daughter? Why did I hate Adam so much, and his people?

He kept staring in the mirror the whole time, facing up to all the personal crimes he'd committed over the years in pursuit of his career, and his ego. He finally gathered together enough strength to go and confront his daughter. Entering her room, she could see how *humbled* he was.

He sat down next to her on the bed and she put her shoulder around him to comfort him. no word passed between them, she knew he was sorry, and he knew she had forgiven him.

Her phone buzzed. Another SMS from Adam. It was the big night.

Chapter 22

Scene 1 – Adam Sings at the Contest

Apologising is more often than not painful for both parties. More so when neither side has an interest in apologising. In that unenviable circumstance, the words are *drawn* out of one's mouth, tattered and meaningless. That's what happened to Richard. He had to utilise broken words that barely slid off his wobbly tongue. "Forgive me," he said. "I hurt you, I know. But I'm not the old me, the one who raised you and loved you and would do anything to make you happy. My ambitions got in the way, for all those years. I'd buried my conscience. Please forgive me, your poor father."

The tears were streaming out of her eyes like raindrops in a storm. She hugged him gently while he stroked her golden curls. He kissed on her cheeks, clearing away the tears. Adam's image came to her at that instant, accompanied by a renewed sense of hope.

Then she remembered the SMS.

She rushed to the TV set to turn it on. Her father couldn't understand what was so important. Then Monica asked if it was the talent contest. Nancy said yes and that Adam was one of the finalists, so Richard said, "Then why watch it here. Wouldn't it be better to go there and cheer him in person!"

"Oh daddy," Nancy flew up in the air like a ballerina that had sprouted butterfly wings. Monica almost couldn't believe her ears.

They raced to get dressed and stuffed themselves in the car.

They only just got there in time to catch Adam's show, everyone on the edge of their seats, not least the judges.

There were four judges, two men, two women. They were eyeing carefully. One finally said, "Please introduce yourself. Name, age, and who is here with you."

"My name is Adam -----," he said with confidence. "I am 22 years old, from Brooklyn. I'm here with my aunt Sarah and my uncle Robert."

Another judge, "And your song?"

"The lyrics are my own. I composed the tunes. I wrote it for the girl I love, and who loves me, despite the colour of my skin. Her father stood in our way so I wrote these words for her, and for him. To know that nothing in the world can keep me from her. I compromised on my love, at first, but I was wrong. You can't love unless your head is held high. So I dedicate this song to everyone who is like me, the wretched of the earth who can't be with the ones they most cherish."

He practically sang those words, in a romantic voice that could have turned stone soft.

Adam had certainly left an effect on the audience, that hushed itself silent in anticipation for what came.

Come back to me, sweetheart
I'm ablaze in the cruel night,
Tortured by my loneliness
Are you still in pain,
On your bedspread
Your picture haunts
Kills me a thousand times
I weep like a child for his mother
Come to me, to cry on your shoulder
Let me pour my worries,

*A thousand times
So that my heart can remain in one piece
My love, you are everything
My world entire
Everything I carry between my shoulders from your love
Come back me
A butterfly that flaps its wings round a light
Ready to extinguish itself, around your light
Come to me so I can kiss away my pains
Let me pour my words from your soul
Words filled to the brim with your passion,
Sprouting from a love that pours over you
Pours over a world hungry
For the taste of your lips, your sparkling eyes
Because you are my inspiration, lying in every atom of my being
Even my own words, sprout from you
Your light, burning behind your eyes
Come back to me, before my heart
Turns into a melted mountain of ice, burned into oblivion by the sun
Desiccated ruins, thrown to the winds
Like snowflakes of dust
Come back to me, gather me together again
I'm lying all over the place
No one but you holds the secret to my resurrection*

So please come back to me and bring me back to life once more
To return as I once was, signing your tune
Words that raise me from the dead
Once more

The audience was aghast, overwhelmed, tearful and ecstatic all at the same time. They could feel his pain. His pain for losing Nancy, and his pain as an orphan. He sang with every part of his soul, his face speaking volumes. The crowds couldn't take it anymore. They gave him a standing ovation, the sound of their clapping tearing through the hall and shaking its walls to their foundations. Monica, Nancy and Richard had to fight their way to where Adam was. Where Sarah and Robert were now.

Nancy finally made it through the throngs of fans, rapping her arms around his handsome neck. She was clinging on so hard it made it difficult for him to bow in appreciation to the audience. It didn't take long for them to figure out that this was his sweetheart that he'd been denied for so long, the symbol of his plight as a black man after all these years. Next came Monica and Richard.

Then the skies above him began to shower snowflakes on him, Nancy still by his side. Golden snowflakes. He'd won. He'd become a finalist, winning the golden bell.

He looked around in desperation, trying to find the panel of judges. He found that there were standing and clapping themselves. Everything he'd been through had been rewarded that night. Fate was finally reconciled to his presence in this world.

Sarah kissed him on his cheek and whispered into his ear how proud she was of him, only for Richard to interject. "Don't waste time. It's time to celebrate, at our place."

Scene 2 – Junior's Pains Increase

John Jr. had lately been frequenting his doctor more and more. His chest pains were on the up, along with feelings of exhaustion and pains and swelling in his legs. That's when the doctor had to level with him and tell him that sex was out of the question. (He laughed, having known this all along). His heart wouldn't take it. He also had to have heart surgery as soon as possible. The longer they waited, the less chance there was to fix the deformity in his heart.

But he was stubborn and refused to go to the hospital, putting on a façade of confidence and strength in front of his friends and employees. It couldn't last. He finally had to go. He was now in a hospital bed, awaiting his fate. Lying there, reminiscing on his life, he found sadness outweighing the pain in his chest. He had everything. Wealth, intelligence, good looks, and it all had come to nothing. He'd been denied the pleasures of women, turning him into a monk that saw a woman as a spirit devoid of a body, free-floating in the heavens, enshrouded in light.

Kevin knew about his brother's deteriorating state. It was the opportunity he needed. He called Steve.

Mere seconds passed before Liz contacted him. She was crying over the phone. She begged him to come to the hospital. Her son wanted to see him.

He couldn't believe it. Why would John Jr., his arch nemesis, *want* to see him?

Liz began sobbing violently. She could see her son slipping away from her in front of her very eyes.

What choice did he have?

When he finally got to the hospital, and room 24 where John Jr. was, he found Ray as well as Liz there. Beyond them was John Jr. he was looking at him, a weak smile on his lips. He reached out to Kevin and Kevin responded by giving him his hand. He grabbed hold and shook it warmly, then pulled him down to sit on the side of the bed.

"Hallo, brother," he said weakly. "I'm so happy you're here. This may be the last time we meet." He paused for a moment, eyes looking out into the distance, before continuing. "I remember, when I was a child, that dad would always tell me that I had a brother named Kevin, in New York. He'd tell me everything about you. How I longed to see you. So we could play and have fun together."

He breathed heavily then went on. "I grew up alone, you see. When I grew on, I kept telling dad over and over again, begging him, to take me with him to New York. One time he did take me there, but he wouldn't let me meet you. But I did see, you from a distance. And I took this picture." He handed Kevin his mobile phone.

Kevin was shocked to find a photo of himself, spliced with a photo of John Jr. It was the screensaver for his mobile. Like they were standing together and were the best of friends.

"The day they read out the will," John Jr. went on. "I wanted to hug young, so we could comfort each other with dad passing away. That's all I wanted. Nothing else. Not the will, not anything." He paused for a moment. "I'm leaving this world, Kevin. Maybe today, maybe tomorrow. Bu I know my days are numbered. I just want you to know, to remember, that I never hated you or wanted anything from you. You know why? Because you're my brother, the son of my father John Meir."

Kevin didn't know what to feel. He got up and raced out of the room, confused. He still had John Jr.'s mobile in his hand.

That's when he received a call from the company lawyer. He insisted that he had to come to his office, right now.

Scared, Kevin raced to the company. He thought something had happened to the company. He found Edward at the doorsteps of the company. Was it that urgent? What could possibly have happened?

He greeted him and took him to his office. After sitting down behind his desk, Edward took out a folio, handing it to Kevin.

He looked through it, uncomprehending. His mind was too numb with fear and confusion. Finally Edward put him out of his misery and explained. John Jr. had handed over all his assets in the company, in his own last will and testament, to his brother Kevin. Everything was like it was before their father had died, as if John Jr. had never existed.

He couldn't respond, he couldn't think. Then he remembered Steve. He'd actually hired someone to kill his own brother, his flesh and blood, and the boy had gifted him with this instead.

Steve!

He rushed out of the room and called Steve. The hit was off. For once in his life his conscience had awakened. He tried and tried to call him, but he wasn't answering on the other end.

What had happened? Was it too late? What could he do?

He was actually afraid for his brother. He thought of him as his brother.

Then the phone rang shaking his hand and knocking him out of his trance. It was Steve.
He tried to talk, tell him to call it off, but Steve was trying to talk back at the same time.
Finally Kevin listened.
"No need, my friend. Your troubles are already over."
"You mean…"
"He died in his bed, after surgery. Didn't even get a chance to get near him. You can rest easy now."
Then Steve's ears were greeted with something he couldn't imagine.
Tears. Kevin was crying.
Steven closed the line. He got paid either way. He didn't have time for people with second thoughts.
Kevin returned to the hospital, forcing himself to go back there. He saw Ray coming out of the room where John Jr. had been. Sandy was there too, trying to console Liz.

Looking into Ray's eyes, he knew now what his friend had known all along that this would happen, that John Jr. had never been greedy and envious. He couldn't afford to be. He knew his days were numbered. He'd confessed to Ray and begged him to keep it a secret.

It was then and there that Kevin realised the full magnitude of what he had lost. He'd wanted a brother growing up too. His father was always too busy with work. His mother too busy with socialising. And he'd squandered it all, that golden opportunity, through his greed and arrogance, assuming everyone was just as he was.

Now his heart ached for the brother he'd never had.

Chapters 23

Scene 1 – Junior's Death and Will

Ray's mind was still overflowing with memories about his friend John Jr., what he'd told him shortly after the reading of his father's will at the company headquarters. How he had terminal heart sickness and how he didn't know long he had in this world, and how he'd asked Ray – begged him – to keep this all a secret.

That's when John Jr. had told Ray about his own last will and testament, and how he was going to hand over his entire share in his father's company back to Kevin. He said that he'd deposited the will with the company lawyer. He asked Ray, again, to keep this all a secret and only tell Kevin after the reading of the will.

Ray tried to talk him out of it, tried to convince him that he was fine and shouldn't be afraid of dying, but Junior would have none of it. He was trusting Ray with everything, and Ray had to oblige him.

Junior's words still rang in his ears, after all this time. The only thing that jolted him back to the here and now way finding Kevin entering his office at the company, the tears of regret still in his eyes.

"So, do you know what really happened now?" Ray said. "Did Edward tell you?"

Kevin now understood that Ray had known all along. He didn't feel betrayed, however. Ray was just being Ray, ever the loyal friend.

"He never wanted anything from you," Ray added.

Kevin clenched his fist and rammed it into the wall, the guilt bearing down on him.

Liz was still in the hospital, sedated, collapsing after her son's death.

Ray, Sandy and Kevin made their way to her after she came to. Kevin looked like a broken man, even she could see that.

They remained with her for the longest time, until she could be safely discharged. Ray and Sandy took her at her own apartment while Kevin eventually headed home to be with Sarah.

He looked sick. Sarah didn't need to be a doctor to see the state her husband was in. "What is it Kevin?"

He was barely able to remain standing. Head held low, she helped him into their bedroom where he threw himself on the bed.

"What is it," she begged.

"My brother, Junior…," his voice trailed off.

She couldn't believe it. He'd called John Jr. his brother, what possibly could have happened?

He continued, "He's dead."

"What did you say?" Sarah couldn't believe it, but from the look of defeat on Kevin's face, she came to see that it was true. "Died? Died how?

That's when Kevin broke down and cried.

She put her arms around him to cradle and comfort him, but even she couldn't control herself and wept as she tried to steady herself.

"The way I treated him," he said with regret. "The way I treated everybody. Mike, Adam." He felt silent for a moment than said, "Adam. Adam? Where is my son? Where is Andy? Adam is going to win the award and be a success and my son, my own flesh and blood, is locked up in Rehab."

He closed his eyes as he fell silent for a second time, hoping in earnest that he would never open his eyes again and go peacefully into the night

Scene 2 – Kevin after his Brother's Death

The night finally passed and a rainbow emerged in the sky following a little drizzle in the early morning. All the residents of the Meir mansion woke up that day and went to the funeral to say their farewells to John Jr.. All except Catherine who was now as comatose as her late husband.

Kevin made sure to have his brother buried in the family burial plot. Only close friends and family were in attendance. After the ceremony Liz made her way to leave, wanting to be by herself for the rest of her life. But Kevin stopped her.

"Where do you think you're going," Kevin said as he apprehended her. "You're living with us, mother."

He startled Liz, first with his request, and second with the word mother. Then he hugged her, startling her a third time.

"I'm… going back to California," she said weakly. "There's nothing for me here."

"You have everything here. You're living with us, at the mansion. You're part of the family now."

"But Catherine…" she tried to protest.

"You're my second mother," he said.
She succumbed to his wishes. What else could she do? She was too broken to say no. she desperately needed her son by her side, and Kevin was giving her a second chance.
She left him take her by the hand.
She sat beside Sarah in the car as Kevin drove them to the mansion.

Scene 3 – Andy Plots his Escape
It was midnight, practically the only time where there was a little peace and quiet in this place that was built and decorated like a Medieval torture chamber. Andy was looking out the window at the world beyond, eyed glazed over, dreaming of getting out of here.
Early next morning he began to execute his plan, as the fog made its way over the ground towards is prison.
He took advantage of the remaining gloom and scaled his way down the walls of the Rehab centre, like a cat thief using the piping as a ladder. He was lucky. The guard at the front gate was sound asleep, not paid enough to remain vigilant at this time of day.

Andy was in a terrible state, having become as thin as a reed, with pale, vampiric skin and a stoop to his back. He kept glancing behind him to make sure no one was there. By instinct he returned to his home, the Meir mansion. He still had the keys to the place, especially the backdoor.

The guard here was also asleep, an old man they kept on duty after all these years of presumed loyalty and diligence. It was 7am and everyone was deep in sleep, so Andy crept up into Catherine's room. He knew that his grandmother wouldn't start an alarm or scream or anything, in her current state. He collected everything he could stuff into his pockets, gold trinkets and jewellery. It was an easy catch, but his state of mind and body didn't help him. he bumped into things and made an unnecessary racket.

That's what alerted Sarah. She woke Kevin up and told her what she'd heard.

He got up, armed himself, and went to see what was going on. This wasn't the first time they'd been robbed. But nothing prepared him for this. Seeing his son, in the state he was in, was shock enough. Let alone what he was carrying with him. Kevin didn't say a word, didn't make a threat, didn't even blink, but Andy panicked and made a run for it, knocking his father over, down the stairs.

He fell and fell, all the way down to the bottom of the stairwell in the Meir mansion, lying there like a corpse.

"Andy, Andy," came Sarah's shouts. She couldn't believe her own eyes.

He didn't listen and ran, like a broken arrow. Sarah then saw what happened to Kevin and ran to him

Liz had woken up too, from all the noise, hearing Sarah crying, holding her husband face as it bled. Liz didn't hesitate and called the ambulance.

Kevin entered the operating room, knocked out cold from the blow to his head. Hours and hours passed, Sarah and Liz in agony, waiting outside the room in a living hell.

The doctor came out and told them that they had been able to save his life, but that Kevin would have to spend the rest of his days in a wheelchair. Sarah was too stunned to respond. Only her eyes spoke in silence for her with the language of tears. Liz cried and cried, like she had over he own son when he had died in this same hospital.

Now Liz became Sarah's mother, holding her up from the shock, driving her home at the end of the day, taking Fran's place after all these years.

Sarah spent the hardest night of her life, arms wrapped around her knees in bed, about what had happened to Kevin and what had happened to Andy. She's lost both on the same day, one an addict and now a criminal, the other paralysed for life. She stared outside the widow to the cold, black world beyond and prayed and prayed till the sunlight pocked its tentative rays through the glass. Then and only then was she prepared to get up and leave, with Liz's help, to the hospital to see if Kevin could come back home with them.

At the hospital, she took the doctor to where they could be by themselves and asked him something that was bothering her. Even with the trauma she knew from her medical experience that her husband shouldn't be paralysed as a consequence of such a fall, as severe as it was.

The doctor concurred. His only answer was that there was more than nerve damage. Some psychological shock, like a guilty conscience, was just as responsible for Kevin's predicament as the fall. But he couldn't comment further. He handed her the medial report and left. She read through it, tears from her eyes falling onto the paper and staining it.

Kevin still couldn't come home. He was still unconscious and under observation. Sarah had to look at him through the glass window in the door of his room. He seemed so far away, she couldn't bare it.

Later in the day Ray came. He already knew what had happened but the company was in an emergency and he felt he owed it to Kevin to stay put and keep the company afloat. The shares that John Jr. had bought were sinking and fast. The company could sink with it.

When he finally got there he kept what was going on from Sarah. She had enough troubles to deal with.

Days passed and Kevin began to recover. In a few days they let him out of bed and into the wheelchair, and the day after that he was able to return to the mansion. Ray continued to run the company in his absence, he didn't know what he was going to tell him. After all Kevin had been through, losing this, his one last hope, could kill him.

Then a miracle happened. The prices rose. Rose by 60%, almost all in one go.

John Jr.'s gamble had paid off, his final gift to his brother. Kevin needed to hear this. Ray made his way to the mansion to give him the good news. Any news at this point was good news.

Kevin couldn't believe it at first. How could this happen? He was no businessman, that was for sure. John Jr. had been right about that.

Then Kevin began to discuss the company with Ray and how he would manage it, if he could manage it, in his current state. But he *had* to, and he had to learn the tricks of the trade. He owed it to his father, and he owed it to his brother.

He made preparations but there was one more thing he had to do.

He told Sarah to come and see him in their bedroom. He asked her to sit down for what he had to say.

Chapter 24

Scene 1 – Kevin's Confession
"A secret," Sarah prompted Kevin.
He nodded. "Yes," he said, tears in his eyes. "I was planning to kill Junior. My brother, who gave me back everything he took. The man responsible for saving my company, my father's legacy." He fell deathly silent for a moment. "Can you believe that I would do such a thing? I couldn't believe it. But I did, and I'll never forgive myself."

"That's enough," Sarah managed to say. "You had no hand in his death, and you'd suffered enough."

She'd had enough too. After what Andy had done, nothing else mattered. He'd crippled his father and ruined his own life.

She comforted Kevin and helped him out of the chair and into bed. He needed to sleep if he was to heal.

Later that night she left for Adam's. The finals of the talent contest just round the corner.

"What song are you doing to sing this time," she asked.

"I'm like you, a human," Adam replied.

What did he say, Sarah asked herself in silence. Where had she heard that expression before? She racked her brains, remembering. It was so long ago. What Mike had told Kevin. The same sentence. "Whose song is this," she finally asked.

"My song. What do you mean," Adam asked, not understanding her question.

"Where did you hear these words before," she persisted.

"Nowhere. I made them it up. Why do you asked," he replied.

"But where did you get the idea from?"

"Nowhere. It's my idea from start to finish," he explained. "I don't understand."

"Your father…," her voice trailed off. "You're saying, what your father said. His own words"

He was stunned, and overjoyed. "I'm my father, mum," he said.

He was more than an extension of Mike. He was Jessica and Fran too. All those memories, overwhelmed Sarah at that moment, just as the tears overwhelmed her eyes.

Robert was in the kitchen during this conversation. Brewing coffee for all of them. He came into the living room as Adam read out the words to Sarah.

Robert saw her crying. He put down the tray and held her hand and squeezed it gently. "I know that past is hurting you, and what happened to Andy. But that's enough."
"Where is Adam?" she finally said.

Scene 2 – Andy at the Police Station
Andy was hiding out in Harlem straight after he ran away from his own house, with the gold and jewellery. He knew this was the place to pawn off his ill-gotten gains, but he wasn't a professional criminal and he wasn't used to rubbing shoulders with the low life that prowled the streets of this neighbourhood. He was wracked with fear, imagining things that weren't thee, like people following him and sounds chasing him. Then he saw his own shadow and made a run for it, and kept running and running as long as he legs would take him.

He found himself in Manhattan. He slowed down and found a jewellery shop and tried to sell what he'd stolen there. The proprietor eyed him suspiciously. Andy was shaking all over, especially his hands, and he was drooling. The withdrawal symptoms were getting the better of him, and the man guessed correctly that this unusual visitor was a junkie. And when Andy agreed to sell it all for a paltry price, he became certain that the man was a criminal and a naïve one at that.

He asked Andy to wait a bit while he got the money, then promptly called 911. He got back but found ways to slow down the conversation till the police came in and arrested Andy.

They deposited him in the squad car, handcuffs on, as the realisation of what was happening to him slowly seeped in. It began with shock and ended with regret.

At the police station Andy called his mother. He couldn't think of anything else to do. She got there as soon as she could, cursing her luck to have given birth to someone like Andy.

After getting there, rushing towards him only to see him sitting down in front of the desk of the officer in charge of his case. The officer in charged had figure out just who Andy was and so was willing to stretch the rules a bit and not throw the boy behind bars, where he deserved to be.

"Could you tell me, again…," the officer tried to ask Andy.

"They're mine. My mother's," Andy said quickly.

Sarah nodded and repeated her son's answer. "I gave them to him," she explained. As angry as she was at him, she couldn't abide to see him in prison.

"Can you corroborate any of this," the officer asked causally. "Can you confirm the jewellery is yours?"

"I can describe them for you," Sarah said.

The officer grinned. He'd expected as much. "Even so. Your son is still going to prison,"

"Why," Sarah asked, perplexed.

"We also found narcotics on him," he explained jovially. "I seriously doubt that you loaned him those as well."

Sarah fell silent. There was nothing more she could do for her son, at least here in the station. She would call the family lawyer and hope for the best, if the news didn't kill Kevin first.

Adam didn't have an inkling any of this was going on. Sarah had left Robert's place and didn't explain where she was going. Right this minute he was with Nancy, rehearsing his big night on the last day of the talent show. Also there was his trainer, James.

"So, what song have you chosen," James asked expectantly. "Hope it's a popular one. Anything someone famous sang to guarantee you win the audience over."

Adam sighed. He didn't want to disappoint his musical mentor, but he'd already made is mind up on the lyrics. "I'm afraid not. I'm going to sing something I wrote myself. And I think it is what's going to win the audience over."

"I trust you talent, but it's an unnecessary risk," James replied.

"I put everything I am into the words," Adam explained.

"I'm sure you did." He moved closer to him to put his hand on his shoulder. "But this is your one shot. You're going to risk your whole career. It's not worth it. Play it safe."

"I wouldn't be me if I did that," Adam replied.

James shook his head. "Well, just tell me the words anyway."

Adam did as he was told, with transparent glee.

After he was finished, the man hugged Adam, thanking him over and over again. "I take back everything I said. That's incredible. You dreamed up all these words by yourself?"

Adam nodded proudly.

"Then we're going to take the world by storm," James proclaimed.

His trainer changed everything, to perfect every single word in Adam's song, the whole routine and the tunes and the performance. They discussed the set decorations at length too, James eager to get Adam's input on everything.

By the end of it James was confident that his student had outstripped his teacher.

Nancy looked on in awe.

The days passed quickly as they took photographs and carefully designed the background for the stage. Sarah wanted to join in herself, but she was too preoccupied with trying to get Andy out of prison. She called Nancy all the time instead, which is when Nancy told her that there was one other contestant that she was worried about. A girl named Jennifer.

Scene 3 – The Finals Loom

The satellite and cabal channels were all plugged into this event, covering every contest and beaming the message to the entire country. Adam was luckier than most. He'd already won the sympathy of his own people in Brooklyn. Everyone was watching, everyone was united, whatever their backgrounds and origins, watching the TV sets in the cafes and coffee shops and public squares across the country. The populations of Brooklyn, Bedford, Christin Coast----, Broom Hill, Park Slope, Fort Green. All were rooting for him. They'd felt his pain, his sincerity, when he spoke from his heart about Nancy and what he'd gone through for her. And he was one of them after all, one of their sons.

Chapter 25

Scene 1 – Contest Day

Tuesday 5th November, it was. The big day. Adam had memorised the date for as long as he could remember. Time to stand up against the crowds. The hall was jam-packed, and that was putting it lightly. People from Brooklyn especially, Adam's fans, and beyond. All eyes were on the stage. Jennifer went on first. She did her routine, while Adam sweated on the inside and outside. Nancy and Sarah were on either side of him. They'd ---- in the meantime. His parents, Mike and Jessica, had bought it originally for Sarah and Sarah now passed it down to her real son Adam. It had the initials of his parents on and he took it warmly and out it on as a good luck.

Nancy and Sarah both hugged and kissed him before heading out into the crowds to take their seats. Monica, Richard, Robert, Sandy and Ray were there too. Kevin was at home watching the TV set, Liz by his side, holding his hand. Jessica completed her song and the audience hushed as the figures were tabulated, then the hallway went dark in preparation for the next and final act.

Nancy caught her breathe in that instant, while Sarah's mind went to her other son, Andy. Her translucent eyes were like giant mirrors, reflecting everything that went on in her. She was looking inward, with her soul, while the audience looked on in the gloom to the stage that was being refurbished for Adam's act. They had taken Andy away, in chains, to jail and she had been powerless to do anything about it. Andy seemed so far away, in her vision, fading out as the lights came back on.

Adam climbed onto the stage like a superstar, lights falling on him like crosshairs. Andy's image came back to haunt her.

Adam began a tap dance, the pleasant sounds reminding her of the clicking and clanging of Andy's chains. While the audience followed his every move, Sarah felt as if her mind had been split between two images. One of Adam on the stage and the other of Andy behind bars.

She was happy and sad, driven to cry and to laugh torn between her two boys.

It was more than anyone could handle. She felt things no poet could express, no matter how eloquent his verse. Her only consolation was that the crowd was falling in love with Adam, and she was being carried away in the wave of appreciation. A star was being born, and everybody knew it. The future was here, the only consolation for the past.

The judges began pelting questions at Adam, about who he was and who had accompanied him here. It helped Sarah focus back on Adam. "All my family, everyone I love, who means something to me, is right here in this room," Adam said proudly. "The whole of Brooklyn is my family." The audience clapped for that one. They really were his family, and he was their son.

"Sweet words, young Adam," said one of the judges. "Let's see if your lyrics are as moving."

"I'm like you, a human being," Adam said, proclaiming the title of his song to the judges and audience and anyone who would hear him. "I dedicate it to everyone who has suffered, and fought back. For everyone who fought for his dignity and didn't say no. I dedicate it to my people, my race, and to every free man who has fought for the freedom and dignity of others."

At that last word, the music began to play. He concentrated, getting ready to unleash himself. In that split second before the words began to fly out of his mouth, he recollected everything he'd read in his life about those before him who had fought against slavery and discrimination, those who had wrote about and championed those heroes, like Alex Hailey and Laurence Hill. It was at that moment that he understood, that he felt just how much his father had suffered. He recollected his own sufferings, for Nancy. But the pains dissipated thanks to all of the merciful hands that had helped him his whole life. Sarah and Robert most of all, his true parents.

The sadness that had tinged his features for the briefest of moments melted away as he began to sing with every fibre of his body. A cast iron voice enlaced with the sweetness of romance and passion:

The words shiver my soul
My sorrows burst asunder
My screams let go
For I still suffer and endure
Because I'm a man who feels
Breathes and speaks and loves
My veins filled with blood
As red as yours
For I'm a human being, like you
But you deny me, my humanity,
Imagine that I am made of stone,
Imagine that I can't feel
Can't imagine that my blood runs red like yours
That I have water in my veins instead
I'm a man, like you, the same breed
One of the few who remain of your victims
Died in the struggle
For me and for you
My most memorable moments, a mirage
My life, a map of sorrows
Blotting out the rays of the sun
My sun, embraces the cloud

The gloom takes over
I stumble and fall in the darkness of my life
A blindman who dreams of the light
Not to fall on the path
My heart overflows with sufferings that know no bounds
But I have no choice, I must love you
I live like a child, naive
Simpleminded and pure
Who loves life to the fullest

The words unreeled like the images of the screen behind him, with the likes of Martin Luther King and Nelson Mandela and Malcolm X, Rose Bryes and ----- Angela Davies. Pictures of firey speeches by these heroes, and images of slavery and suffering and riots. Then images of the black youths in Dallas, embracing the policemen in peace.----
The audience was taken along this journey, the history of the suffering of the black man, all juxtaposed with Adam's operatic voice and his own pains, choreographed to perfection. Word and image and music. The audience rose and fell with the pitch of his tortured voice, on the verge of tears, at every juncture of the history on display.

At every juncture, came Adam's words, "I am like you, a human."

Tears escaped his own eyes as he sang, piercing the hearts of the audience in the hall, the viewers at home, and listeners everywhere. There was no escaping that passion on display, and Adam was at the centre of the emotional storm he had unleashed, swept up like his own listeners.

One of those watching was Kevin, a man beaten down by everything he had cherished. His mother betraying the memory of his father, his father the sanctity of his marriage, him betraying his wife with Janet and then betraying his brother, repaid finally with Andy's betrayal. Adam's voice echoed along the walls of the mansion that was now Kevin's prison. "Forgive me, Adam," he said to himself. "Forgive me, Mike. I was cruel to you for no reason."

Liz squeezed his hand. She was the only other person there in this barren, hollow place. Apart from poor Catherine and their maid Rita, who took care of her.

"I am like you, a human," the audience began to chant.

Sarah, Nancy, Robert, Ray and the others chanted along with them, tears in their eyes. Then Adam's session came to an end, and Jennifer remerged. The hall went deathly silent as the counting began.

In the background, a TV presenter could be heard, her stiletto heels clanking away on the floor beneath her sleek and sexy legs.

The judges began smiling and trading pleasantries with Jennifer and Adam, pouring more fuel on the tensions of the audience and contestants alike. Finally a woman entered the picture, holding an envelope in her hand. The name of the winner was inside. Adam and Jennifer held their breathes in anticipation. Instead of announcing the winner and putting them all out of their misery the woman talked about the contest and its history and the stages of the contest and the names of all the contestants, and so on and so forth.

People in the audience began hooting and shouting. They wanted the result already. They couldn't take any more of this dillydallying. The lady ignored them, and began talking about the sheer size of the ash prize. A million dollars, as well as the fame that would follow and the distribution f the winner's CD, all expenses covered, nationwide.

The people at home and out at the cafes and bars began shouting themselves at the prorogued torture.

Then the moment finally came as the envelope was opened.

Tears this time, from Robert and Nancy and Sarah, but tears of joy.

They couldn't restrain themselves, rising up from their seats and heading t the stage to embrace their son, Adam, the winner.

Those who hadn't understood Adam's words, whether here in the hall or at home, understood finally when they saw three white people embracing a black man. The audience itself as divided between black and whites, as if the residents of the south and north from the dark days of civil war were back and reconciled with the birth of this new young star named Adam.

Now fans were rising to the podium themselves, asking for autographs or desperate to be photographed with the winner.

Among the crowd was none other than Richard. "Adam's won. We've got to celebrate. Celebrate my daughter's future husband. The son I never had, Adam!"

He said it with such pride. Sarah interjected and asked that the party begin at Fran's house, starting tomorrow, where Adam's parents had lived the happiest days of their lives. Then move to Richard's house.

When Sarah got home, she found Kevin waiting for her. "You were always right," he said.

She held his hand, she knew he wanted to apologise for all the hate he'd felt and how he had hurt Mike and Adam, and even Junior. But there was no need. He'd been through enough, paid back enough.
"God forgives all," she finally said.

Scene 2 – The Party

The following day was all celebration. Sarah went back to her home in Flat Bush, deserted for so long. She took her fill of the street in which her old home lay, reminiscing on everything that she had gone through here, good and bad, from her earliest days till her marriage day when she had left, only to return again and again. She took her key out and unlocked the door, unlocking a door in her own mind at the same time.

Entering, she found the house as it always was. Every corner held a memory. The smell of Jessica ad Fran and Mike were still there. Their pictures on the walls. There was only one thing missing. The yellow butterfly. She sighed in relief. Their spirits were finally free.

Not long after, the place was ready to greet the guests and the guests began flocking there. There was so much to celebrate. It wasn't just Adam's victory. It was the consummation of his marriage with Nancy too.

The place, deserted and empty for so long was brimming with activity and voices and laughter, a fitting tribute to where she had grown up. Happiness would forever rest in this place as it came to life once more.

The linking of champagne glasses soon followed after, but there was one more surprise in order. Kevin made his entrance. Liz by his side, helping him with the wheelchair.

He apologised for being late!

"No more apologies," Sarah replied knowingly.

Adam added, "You're here now, with your family."

Kevin, adamant, said, "You were always better than me, Adam." Tears slipped from his eyes as he spoke.

Someone handed him a cup full of punch, a victory toast. He drank and became one of them, the people he'd never wanted to rub shoulders with.

Richard and Monica stood close to the fireplace and the ----- , drinking their own glasses of punch. Behind it the portrait of Fran. Robert's eyes were transfixed on it, blotting out everything else in the party, his memories flowing along with the soft tunes of the music. Sarah began to introduce the place to Kevin, her happy memories in this corner and that corner, while Ray and Sandy made it there, along with some of their own friends. That's when the party really got started, with dancing and merriment, with Adam taking Nancy to one side and kissing.

He placed his hand over her belly. He could feel the baby now.

Beyond them, Kevin had eyes for Adam alone. The son he never had. The real son who would honour his parents no matter what, the boy he had deprived of his mother. He tried to lift his hand, with difficulty, towards Adam. He noticed.

Kevin was pointing. The people all turned to see him. They could see the pain he was in, the sheer physical agony, that he braved so he could say, over and over again:

I am like you, a human.
I am like you, a human...

Made in the USA
Middletown, DE
26 August 2020